½ Priced Murder

Written by Ardis K Mani

Cover Art by Gail Osterberg

For all of the amazing people
I've worked with
who keep the retail world afloat.

Chapter 1

The trail of beet juice reminded her of blood. Where the garbage bag had rested for a mere five seconds, a pool of it had seeped from a rip in the plastic bag and hazardly sat in a bumpy circle on the cement floor. From this, drag marks could be clearly seen leading through the set of heavy, swinging doors of the Receiving Area, continuing all the way past the back door, the hump of the store's box crusher which stuck out from the building awkwardly, the employee smoking area, and ten feet of slush strewn pavement to where the heavy load was swung clumsily into the gaping maw of a dumpster.

The girl wiped her hands together, thinking that was that, until she turned and was faced with the glaring evidence of what looked to be an attempted homicide. "Damn it," she cursed bitterly under her breath, then quickly made her way inside to start cleaning everything up before someone slipped and broke something—maybe even died for real.

When she entered the store one of her co-workers was coming by with a mop bucket and grinned evilly as she teased, "Alex, I just knew you would end up killing someone eventually. That face of innocence and friendly demeanor is way too suspicious."

"Yeah, yeah, whatever Cyndi. You're no fairy princess yourself."

"No? Well with all the sugar I inhale in the bakery, some sweetness should have rubbed off by now." Cyndi and Alex both laughed. "Here, this mop is for you."

Alex thanked her and tried to steer the bucket over to

the beginning of the garbage spill. It swerved to and fro, sloshing water here and there. One of the wheels for all three mop buckets was broken, a possible conspiracy, making it difficult to maneuver the yellow devils. While trying to drive the blasted thing, Alex did a quick check list in her head: lights off, counters scrubbed, salads wrapped, windows wiped clean, inventory on the salad bar and meat and cheese cases taken—just need to finish mopping. The morning crew had been talking shit again today—whispering that the night crew wasn't pulling their weight in the department, and Alex wasn't going to let that go—not on her watch! She took great pride in her work, even if she was just a humble deli worker in a small town grocery store.

Cyndi had already closed her department and came over, leaning against the now darkened cheese case. She had ditched the apron and hat, showing off a nice head of blond hat hair. A puffy pink winter coat covered the majority of her uniform; the sequins sewn into the seams sparkling whenever she moved. Overall, Alex wasn't surprised to see her friend in such an outlandish display of winter apparel. They had worked with each other long enough that Alex knew that if it was shiny and pink then Cyndi would grab it. And if it was extra frilly and princess-like, most likely Cyndi's two year old daughter would be forced to wear it.

Gaily, Cyndi asked, "So what are you doing after work tonight? Want to go for drinks? Bradie is at her dad's house this week and so tonight Boy and I are going to 8th Street Ale Haus near 8th and Michigan Ave. You're welcome to tag along."

Alex was about to refuse, but then took a moment to think about it. This was probably the third time since Christmas that Cyndi had been kind enough to invite her to go out with her and her "Boy," and the third time she was going to habitually decline. But there was no one waiting anymore at home and Alex hadn't been out for awhile. Plus, today had been utter hell between the guy who had called in sick and the rude customers who couldn't understand what the term "understaffed" meant—no wonder the night crew wasn't always able to finish the prep lists!

Alex hesitated a second longer then nodded her head, "Okay, sure. Let me finish up, run home quick and change, and then I'll meet you guys there."

Cyndi's face lit up in a smile, "Alright! See you soon!"

Alex finished mopping a few minutes later and did a double check to make sure that everything was turned off before going again to the Receiving Area to put the mop bucket away. As she made her way through the back hallway that wrapped around the sales floor like a skin with only a thin wall in between, weaving around jam-packed U-boats (the beasts of burden of the grocery world used to transport and store extra inventory) toward the mop closet, she noticed a light above one of the makeshift cubicles that served as desks for most of the department heads of the little grocery store.

Everyone but the store manager himself, Nathan (Nate) Bartley, and Jack, the produce manager, had their domain back here snuggled close to the back up dry goods and wine bottles. Nate was lucky enough to get the luxury of a private office up near the front of the store, while Jack had to make room for his invoices and receiving papers amongst the fruits and veggies kept in the produce cooler and adjacent production/packaging space.

But in this rude landscape of the back hallway there was a desk for Joe, the wine and liquor guy, on the right. You could tell which was his by the amount of wine and brandy bottles (unopened of course) that sat clustered around it. Evan from the meat department was directly across from Joe's desk, but his was kept unkempt with paperwork strewn all over the place. Next to Evan's was Julie's desk. She was in charge of customer service and her desk was always neatly organized. A large quantity of family photos was pressed into the surrounding wall with thumbtacks, disguising the fact that it was made of unpainted plywood. A small space which housed a printer and some file cabinets came next, and then the last two desks set across from one another—one for Parker, the grocery manager, and the other for Sean. Sean Ritter was the bakery and deli coordinator and it was his light which was still aglow at this late hour.

As Alex approached she noticed Sean was totally engrossed in whatever it was he was doing with his head bent over some sort of account book, and a pen busily scratching across a notepad. The glow from his active computer screen was casting his features in a bluish hue that made him look surreal, almost ghostly.

"Hi, Sean. I didn't know you were still here," Alex hailed in an attempt to not startle him.

Even with the noise from the mop bucket and her greeting, Sean jerked visibly. "Jesus, you scared me!" Then he laughed shortly to himself. "It's eight already, huh? Well, have a good night, Alex."

Alex replied with a "you too," and finished putting away the mop bucket, watching as the dirty water spiraled down the floor drain, the bloody beet juice now camouflaged with the rest of the floor's dirt and grime from the day's labors. When she walked passed Sean's desk again he didn't even look up. His hand was still busy scrawling secret notes of importance.

Fishing out her car keys from her apron pocket while walking toward the front of the store, the time clock, and her Honda Fit, she thought she heard the buzzer for the back door—the one that rang if someone went outside to smoke or take out their trash and the door unfortunately locked behind them—and hesitated for a moment. Then she remembered that Sean was back there and figured he could get it. Besides, her friends were waiting for her and she needed some friend time. So, repositioning her tote bag that carried her book, money, and punch card more firmly on her shoulder she continued her step toward the time clock and to the cold martini that was long overdue.

Chapter 2

Sheboygan, Wisconsin is 57 miles north of Milwaukee and about 135 miles north of Chicago, skirting the edge of Lake Michigan. The history of the name "Sheboygan" isn't widely known other than the fact that it was a Native American creation referring to the sounds of the Sheboygan River. The Chippewa called this area "shawb-wa-waygun," meaning "wind;" the Potawatomie's version was "shab-wa-wa-going," meaning "rumbling underground;" and Chief Oshkosh called this rugged landscape of dense forest and rivers "sawbe-wah-he-con," meaning "echoes." There's also the white man joke that the name "Sheboygan" came from the exclamation uttered by an Indian brave when he looked at his squaw and newborn and shouted, "She had a boy again!"

No matter how it got its name, Sheboygan became an official Wisconsin city in 1835 and immediately became home to thousands of Germans and Dutch immigrants traveling by lake going vessels from Chicago and Buffalo, seeking religious freedom. With these men and women came a strong German cultural influence that led to the love of music and sports; skills such as woodworking, farming, hunting, and cheese making; and good food. Sheboygan is specifically famous for inventing bratwursts, grilled, and then served on a hard roll. Brat Days is a major summer festival that the locals look forward to each year, along with German Fest, and the Yacht Gala held along the shoreline of the lake.

Today, Sheboygan is still a large manufacturing and farming community. It and the rest of Sheboygan County are home to many high quality resorts, golf courses, beautiful parks and beachfronts—and bars. Not including any restaurants that might serve alcohol, there are 49 bars and pubs within the city limits. Visitors will surely never go thirsty in Sheboygan-town.

After finding a spot to park on the street, Alex left her car and headed toward the Ale Haus. The night air was extra chilly and she was happy that she had grabbed a scarf to wear from her apartment before coming to meet her friends.

When she entered the bar, the quiet winter's night was drowned out by an array of noises: gambling machines set up closest to the doors that spit and dinged out arcade sounds, there were big screen TV's above the bar narrating tonight's news—the sports highlight special, as well as the clamor of voices, of laughter, of drinks being poured, of glasses being clinked together, and of pop music being blasted from unseen wall speakers. Alex looked around at all of the people clustered around the bar and surrounding tables and did a double check that today was still Monday. Normally Monday nights were slow bar nights, but tonight was an exception.

She finally spotted Cyndi's hand waving wildly above her head and made her way over to the tiny table she and her "Boy" were sitting at. "Wow, it's busy here tonight," Alex said as she reached the table. She had to shout to be heard over all of the noise. "Hi, Evan."

"Hello, Alex. How was closing tonight?" It was always weird seeing other co-workers outside of work, especially when they were kind of your boss. And while Evan was the meat manager at Forestgrove Grocery and therefore not Alex's direct boss, it was still a little strange to see him in civilian clothes, let alone go out drinking with him. Evan and Cyndi had been dating for a few months now. They had been able to keep it a secret from everyone else at work (managers weren't allowed to date their underlings and they didn't want their relationship to cause any trouble)—that was, until Alex had caught them kissing in the back hallway one day, just a little peck, nothing more, but enough to prove that something was going on. Alex wasn't bothered by their relationship and had no intention to tattle on them. You couldn't help who you fell in love with, right?

"Work was fine," Alex responded while removing her jacket and other winter accessories. "I'm sure Cyndi already explained how annoyingly busy it was, but otherwise, yeah, everything was fine."

"Apparently it's someone's 21st birthday today," Cyndi smiled and gestured toward the crowd around them before taking a large sip from her already half—downed Cosmo.

"Yeah and at least a few of those guys in the group are cops," Evan added. He didn't seem too happy about that fact, Alex noticed.

Alex glanced back at the large cluster growing along the bar like a cancerous tumor. Shouts of "Drink, drink, drink!" and "Let's do shots next!" could be heard amongst the throng, and for a moment Alex was disgusted. Turning back to the table she sighed, "Well, they are off duty. They can go into bars if they want. I mean, it is a free country."

"Yeah, but apparently cops make Evan nervous," Cyndi glanced mischievously at Evan. "As soon as he learned they were here he wanted to leave, but I told him we couldn't because I had told you we were going to meet here and I left my phone in my car. Besides, I want to order cheese curds! This place serves the best ones in the area, you know."

Evan scratched the back of his neck as he said, "Having police around while I'm trying to relax just doesn't work. I feel like they're never really 'off the job,' you know? Anyways, here Alex, you can have my seat and the first of your rounds is on me for finally agreeing to go out with us," Evan said with a smile. "So, what'll it be?"

"Um, I'll take one of whatever Cyndi's having. That looks good."

Evan nodded, "Alright, one Cosmo coming up. And can I borrow your ID? They card like crazy here unless of course you look fucking ancient."

"Yeah, I don't think my twenty-five years have given me that many gray hairs," Alex laughed as she dug through her purse and finally fished out her ID. "Alright, just don't look too hard at the picture—I had a cold the day they took it."

Evan took the ID from her and waved his free hand in a form of dismissal, "They always make everyone look horrible on their license. Its some sort of rule, or something."

When Evan walked away Cyndi leaned in closer. Alex could tell that she must be a lightweight and that the alcohol was already affecting her because she was a lot gigglier than normal. "After we down these and eat a few cheese curds, let's try to get Evan to go into the gay bar. It's just down the street and I've never been in one before!" Cyndi made a pouty face and then continued, "He says he doesn't want to, but I heard the bartenders there are so hot!"

"But you already have a boyfriend."

"But I can still look, and you don't. We can look for someone for you there, well, maybe not there. They all might really be gay. . . Alright, let's take a look-see here then." Cyndi took a moment to scan the other people and immediately her eyes began to sparkle. "Look at that one right next to the guy wearing the blue sweater. What about him?"

Alex rolled her eyes but did take a look at the prospect Cyndi was trying to point out. He was an okay looking man, probably in his thirties, but he was already starting to go bald. "Too old, hon. Try again."

"Hmm, alright, how about the one near the birthday boy—he's pretty cute."

Alex took another gander. The birthday boy was obvious as he was forced into wearing one of those dumb cone hats with the elastic bands which more often than not snapped before you could secure them beneath your chin. The guy standing next to the birthday boy's stool was pretty attractive though. He was laughing as he pounded the birthday's boys back and then laughed even harder when the foam from his own glass sloshed over the side and onto his skin. He set the glass carefully back on the bar and licked the spilt beer from the back of his hand.

Alex turned quickly away. She was starting to feel uncomfortable. Maybe coming to a bar like this wasn't the best idea after all. "He's nice, really, but I'm not actually in the market for a man right now."

"No? Well, just let me know when you are and I'll help you find the right one," Cyndi winked.

Just then Evan came back carrying Alex's martini and an amber ale for himself. He set both glasses down on the table and then returned Alex's ID. "The curds will be out shortly. We got the order in just in time too. I guess the kitchen closes at ten."

Alex checked her watch reflexively. It read 9:57.

"So where are we going after this? Or do we want to stay here?" Evan asked.

"Its kind of loud here—too difficult to talk," Alex chimed in.

"Bar hoping it is! We can stop at Urbane, Mojo's, and then head over to The Blue Light!" Cyndi said, practically bouncing in her chair.

Evan let out a groan that turned into a smile, "You really want me to go into a gay bar, don't you?"

"Come on!"

Evan and Alex both laughed and then finally Evan caved in, "Well, alright. I guess I have enough confidence in myself as a man to make the journey, but only a quick peek, alright?"

Cyndi beamed and for a moment the two of them were completely oblivious to Alex's presence as they stared into each others eyes. Then Evan broke the stare by kissing the top of Cyndi's head and the two embraced before changing the topic to how wonderful the newly arriving cheese curds looked in their checkered basket.

Alex had to smile at the couple across the table. They were so adorable and they looked great together. They also made a small pocket somewhere deep inside hurt with the emptiness it contained. *For now its enough that I have friends like these that I can turn to for comfort and support,* she told herself sternly. *These two and the other people I've met since working at Forestgrove have become my family, and for that I am most grateful.*

Tuesday, February 1st

Chapter 3

Alex awoke the next morning like she normally did—with the alarm going off at 7:30 a.m. and hitting snooze every five minutes for the next hour and a half. Finally, what actually did prompt her to get out of bed were a full bladder and a cat sticking its whiskers up her nose in search of its breakfast. She kept trying to make herself get out of bed early, but for some reason it never worked. Most of this was due to her difficulties in turning her brain off for the night. Ever since her parents had been killed in a car accident three years earlier, sleep had been difficult. Often she would be awake until midnight or later with random thoughts, obligations, and responsibilities plaguing her exhausted mind; resulting in her failed efforts of greeting the day while it was still young. In her defense this morning, she had been out with Evan and Cyndi till almost 1 a.m..

Finally emerging from her room, with her cat weaving between her legs, Alex began her daily routine. She started the coffee maker, and even though it was just her in the apartment she still made 6 to 8 cups worth of brew. She didn't need it to help ditch a hangover because she never got those no matter how much she drank. She just enjoyed the taste. While the coffee maker sputtered and gurgled to life she fed the anxious tabby, washed yesterday's dishes, poured a bowl of cereal, and snatched the book she was reading from its sack. Then, with a large mug filled with the steaming goodness of pure black Folgers she made her way to the dinning room table to break her fast.

Because she lacked the funds, Alex didn't have Internet. Instead she always brought her iPad to work and used the free wifi the little coffee shop next to the grocery store provided. She also wasn't one for keeping up with current events a.k.a. watching the depression that is the morning news. Anything and everything that was important, she discovered, could be heard from her customers and co-workers, and when all else failed, her Facebook account provided a fair amount of local and global communications; however, if she *had* turned on the news that fateful day, then she would have been prepared for what she would be dealing with in the days to come.

But for the present she enjoyed her peaceful and usual morning routine and at 10:30 on the dot she gulped the last of her coffee and got ready for work. She brushed her teeth, combed her long, brown hair and then tried her best at making it stay as a sophisticated bun (she had always been bad at doing hair) and settled for a messy one instead. She didn't add any makeup—her blue eyes were surrounded by naturally lush and long black lashes, and her lips had always been full and red. Then she donned her black chef's coat and pants, black socks and shoes, and a black cap and apron. The only thing not black was her silver name tag which was pinned to her left breast pocket.

Then, with a quick goodbye to the now contented cat who sat cleaning its forepaws in a sunlit space on the carpet, she re-shouldered her book bag and headed out. In the driver's seat of her Fit, with the garage door open and the car humming, she paused to select a new CD to start the day's adventures. She always loved music, all sorts of styles, and today she was feeling upbeat and ready to take on the world. In such a situation only one band would do. She selected a black and red disc from the assortment that sat in the soft rack attached to the passenger side drop down mirror and slipped the disc into the slot just above the radio dials.

Then, with the beginning measures of AC/DC's *Shoot to Thrill* starting up, she shifted into reverse and went off to hit the highway and start saving the world from starvation one deli sandwich at a time.

Grocery stores themselves have been around as long as man—only they started out as primitive trading posts or market places where tribes of various peoples met to exchange and barter their homemade goods. Delicatessens specifically originated in Europe, but didn't become popular until they came to America in the 1800's. Started up by Jewish immigrants mainly in New York, these small corner shops became wildly accepted during the Great Depression as they produced quality and quantity sandwiches that the populace could afford; the two most popular sandwiches being Reuben's and Lindy's. Overall these Jewish eateries signified the attainment of the American Dream for many people who had come from overseas, and they continue to thrive today in many places.

Although working in a deli might seem like a lame job to some, Alex was proud to carry on such a tradition. She loved staying busy, making the freshest products you could have, and talking to the people who came and went. There was never a dull moment—especially when your deli department was a part of one of the coolest grocery stores in the county!

Forestgrove Grocery, home of adorable and price-cutting Freddy the Ferret, was a mom and pop type of grocery store with a flare for the urbane. It was nestled between an overpriced clothing store and Capital E Chino's Coffee House on the rich side of the Sheboygan, WI tracks, and boasted a fully operational, made-from-scratch deli and bakery department, a spectacular fresh fish display in the meat department, as well as being the place where all of your household goods could be found. The produce was 100% organic, and 40% of all the goods sold were made somewhere in Wisconsin. It was closer to 50% if you did not count the liquor department, the majority of wine labels and hard alcohol being imported.

As Alex took the turn that would have her pass the front of the store and eventually reach the employee parking in the farthest lot, *Thunderstuck* was in mid-play, and after a glance at the old familiar sight of her work place she choked on the familiar lyrics, her heart beating furiously in her throat. For a moment she was genuinely spell bound at the sight of at least a dozen emergency vehicles parked askew in front of the entrance, their lights painting everything red and blue.

Alex took the first empty spot she found to park, then made her way toward the lights. Looking closely she noted that caution tape was roped around the entrance, hung between portable cones to leave enough space for the investigation teams to move about. And even with the brisk February air and the slushy parking lot, a large crowd had gathered behind it. Uniformed police men, standing stoically silent, held the reporters and spectators at bay while others in uniforms of various types kept coming and going.

Alex pushed her way through the mass of people, ignoring the irritated looks and snarls from the others. She had to find out what was going on, after all she worked here! Was there a fire, a gas leak? Was anyone hurt? She tried to look around to see if there was an ambulance present, but the throng was making it difficult to be sure. When she reached the caution tape she saw that one of her co-workers was talking to a policeman not too far away. Someone had dragged over an outdoor table set from the coffee shop so she had somewhere to sit. Tears were streaming down her clearly hysterical face.

"Claire!" Alex cried, and tried to duck under the tape, but an officer was there telling her that she couldn't do that.

However, Claire had heard the call of her name and rushed over, immediately gripping Alex in a hug that was more desperate than warm.

"What's going on?" Alex asked as she stepped, this time unhindered, under the tape.

"I'm sorry. I guess no one called you." There was a long pause while Claire tried to gain the courage to retell her story. When it finally came out, it was in a quick jumble of words, "I was in the freezer getting the morning's bread for the sandwiches since no one stocked it last night, not that it's your fault, but there were boxes all over like some kind of avalanche and he was just sitting there! At first I though maybe he was sleeping or playing some sort of joke—you know how weird he can be sometimes—well he-he wasn't. He . . . Oh God! Alex, he's *DEAD*!"

Alex's eyes widened and her voice was slightly above a whisper when she asked, "Who? Who's dead, Claire?"

Fresh tears started to fill her eyes as she replied with a wail, "Sean. Sean's dead!"

Chapter 4

Detective Aubrey Steiner, age 27, walked slowly down aisle 8, the fluorescent lights reflecting off the pearly waxed floor not helping his hangover one little bit. He passed eggs, bagels, assorted dips and coffee creamers to his left, and milk and assorted refrigerated juices to his right. It was unexpected, early wake-up calls such as this that made him regret staying out so late, but yesterday had been his youngest brother's twenty-first birthday and how else was the boy going to learn how to party properly?

The store's opener had time to do a few things before the body was found, one of them being to turn on the God-awful 90's music that was now pouring out of every speaker in the place.

When winter comes in summer,

when there's no more forever...

that's when I'll stop lovin' you!

"Timberlake this early in the morning? Sorry Justin, I hate to tell you, but I don't need your love, and for at least one (deceased) person here today, there isn't going to be a summer ever again," Aubrey said to himself with a sneer. In his opinion the 90's was a horrible decade for music, and the 2000's hadn't been any better so far.

When he came to the end of the aisle he stepped through a set of swinging doors and entered a hive busy with activity. If death was messy, the clean up is always worse. In this case, the little area that the grocery people called the "Dairy Receiving" (apparently not to be confused with the other, more prominent "Receiving Area" which was much larger and to where most of the trucks delivered) was crammed with various policemen and forensic agents, all busy recording *this*, taking pictures of *that*. Suddenly the amount of paperwork he would have to fill out if this case was indeed ruled a homicide flashed before his eyes, and the pressure in his head increased slightly. He really wasn't a fan of the paperwork aspect of the job.

But maybe today was his lucky day. Initial reports said it looked to be a simple accident, not even an intentional suicide. Maybe the coroner would produce a favorable verdict and all of the witness statements would easily check out so Aubrey would be able to get back in his truck, go home to his cramped apartment, and sleep the rest of the day away.

And maybe pigs could fly.

Producing his badge to the officer standing just outside the door of the large walk-in freezer, Aubrey pulled open the latch and entered the darn thing. He expected that with all of the people coming and going the freezer would be warm, but then he mentally slapped himself. Of course the evidence guys would maintain the temperature as best as they could. Otherwise the corpse might be compromised.

Holding his bare hands under his armpits for warmth, Aubrey approached the three bodies at the far end of the freezer. One was the corpse itself, left in a sort of seated position on the floor, using a frozen butterball for a back cushion. A late-thirty-something, Caucasian, male. Then there was Dr. Florence, kneeling beside the deceased, finishing up his initial autopsy, and Sergeant Mel Clappers, standing patiently beside them both. Aubrey internally groaned. He had nothing against Florence. He had barely worked with the odd, old fellow so far, but Mel was another story. Mel was one of his father's old buddies.

"Hey, Mel, what do we have here?" He tried to sound

sociable. Otherwise he might hear about it later.

"Well, look here—the detective assigned the case finally showed his face and its Steiner's kid!" Mel's grin was all teeth and almost as bright as the waxed floor outside. Also, his handshake was border-line bone-crushing. "I heard you made detective. Congratulations! That's what your daddy always wanted for you. I bet he's so proud. This your first real case? If it is a homicide, that is. I know we don't get too many murders in these parts, other than drunken bar fights. This might be kind of exciting for you—a real mystery—again, if it is a homicide."

"Well, Dr. Florence, is it? Or isn't it?" Aubrey asked bluntly.

Dr. Florence sighed and sat back on his heels. "I'm sorry, but I'm just not sure. I need to take him back to my *slice and dice factory*, boys. I mean, at first glance it looks like this poor fellow froze to death, but. . ." He paused and bent the victim's head forward. While holding back some hair, he pointed with a gloved index finger and said, "back here there seems to be some sort of perimortem cranial fissure. None of the boxes here could make a wound like that, and if he had hit one of the metal racks, there would have been hairs and some blood left behind. Either way, this is a nasty bump which may or may not have done him in."

"Possible murder then, huh?" Aubrey murmured. His eyes clouded in thought, his hangover momentarily forgotten. He would need access to the dead guy's computer, his phone records. What was he doing in the store so late last night? Finishing inventory maybe, or something else? But first he needed to interview the person who found the body, and with a request that he be called once the verdict was sure, he turned away from the coroner and Mel and began checking off his mental checklist. Aubrey knew his motivation had been lacking lately. Maybe a real case was just what he needed to pull him out of his funk. But whether an accidental death or a prompted one, he was still going to have to do a bunch of paperwork. Damn.

Mel shook his head fondly after Aubrey's receding figure and declared humorously to Dr. Florence, "It started when he was first introduced to Scooby-Doo. He started solving the mysteries of the neighborhood and following people's footprints."

Dr. Florence stood up and carefully took off his soiled gloves. "Is that why he wanted to become one of us?"

Mel chuckled, "Couldn't tell you his reasoning, but that kid's got a talent for sniffing out people's dirty underwear just like his old man. He'll find the truth behind this poor frozen fellow, just you wait."

~*~*~*~*~

Sean Ritter, the deli and bakery coordinator of Forestgrove Grocery was found dead on February 1st. His obituary was published on the third of February with a funeral opened to immediate family only. No specific details were released to the public about his peculiar death other than the location, which everyone already knew because of the large degree of gossips in Sheboygan County.

Forestgrove Grocery was allowed to reopen ten days after the incident with much persuasion on the store manager's part. So on the morning of February 9th, Alex was relieved to get a phone call from Mr. Bartley updating her and everyone else who worked there that they could come back to work the next day if they felt up to it. The master schedule was still in a tentative state as he wasn't sure how many people would actually be returning right away, if ever. Apparently a couple of employees had quit. They didn't want to work in a building where someone's soul might still be haunting the halls. . .

For most people, having someone they know die is an unnerving experience, and while Alex was shocked and sad about her ex-boss's death, she wasn't superstitious and was able to shake it off rather easily. They hadn't been close. In fact, she thought he was sexist and kind of mean. He had been in the navy for many years before turning to food service and thought his military tactics were the best way to manage people. They weren't. Most of the time they led to frustration, unneeded stress, and tears.

Her mind drifted back to her first yearly review, when Sean had sat Alex down and told her bluntly that she was too soft as a supervisor for the night crew, and that she let people walk all over her. He said it was okay to be a bitch, as long as you did it with a smile. That wasn't the only inadequate philosophical advice she had had to contend with, but Alex tried her best to smile and nod whenever he was around.

Besides his "charming" personality, Alex was starting to get used to losing people—first her parents, then her high school beau. Losing a jerk manager wasn't such a hard blow. So with a mix of anxiety and excitement, she showed up for work an hour early the next day.

Chapter 5

The first thing Alex noticed as she drove up to the grocery store was that the parking lot was extremely full for a Thursday in the early afternoon. Weren't people in school? At work? She shrugged it off and entered the coffee shop. They were pretty slow. Only a couple stragglers remained at window tables, drinking their brews and reading the papers. Two bodies usually held down the fort during this time of day and today happened to be two of Alex's favorites because they always gave out the best gossip.

Jennifer saw Alex first and greeted her warmly, "Well, Hello there! I haven't seen you in a while. So the store is officially back open then?"

Jennifer was a sweet lady in her fifties who only worked part time while her kids were in school. Otherwise she was a full time stay at home mom. She was also a worry wart and not one to handle stress well.

"Hi Jennifer. Hello Susan. I would like a small hazelnut mocha, please."

Jennifer smiled, "I thought you were trying to give up caffeine?"

Alex mimed a guilty look, "Yeah, that hasn't been working out too well."

Both of the barista's laughed as Jennifer started to measure out the proper amount of espresso needed for the drink and Susan took Alex's money. Jennifer continued talking over her shoulder, raising her voice so it could be heard over the milk steamer as she worked. "That's just crazy about what happened to that Ritter guy, isn't it? Didn't he have two kids too—a toddling boy and a baby girl?"

Alex grunted an unintelligible answer. She had no idea, but Jennifer kept on talking without waiting for a response, "Well he was in here that morning, you know, the day he died? It always bugged me how he would get his large black java and look around the place like he was inspecting it. He would make all of these snide comments—remember Susan-dear? Like, 'If I owned this place, I would do this,' or 'If this was my store, I'd move this here,' or 'I'd change that.' It's really sad though. And Claire, the poor angel, was the one who first saw the body. I bet—" At that point the bells over the door rang again and another customer entered. Jen handed Alex her coffee and gave a note of thanks before turning her attention to the new arrival.

Blowing away the steam, Alex moved to the side, closer to Sue who was busy rinsing off mixing spoons and ceramic mugs. Sue was in her early forties with long, coppery blonde hair and laugh lines starting to form around her eyes. Her husband owned his own company and they were well-off, but Sue continued to work because she loved to interact with people. She was the type of person who didn't miss much.

Sue's voice was just above a whisper when she said, "There's a rumor going around that Sean was murdered. Don't let Jen know. She's wired up enough about the topic as it is. She might just have a heart attack or something if she found that out."

Alex's eyes widened. "Why do you say that?"

"Daniel was over here a little while ago and told us there's a detective just hanging around the place, being escorted everywhere by Mr. Bartley. He's been asking random questions. Also, that same detective was in here very early this morning—I saw his badge when he pulled out his wallet to pay."

"What, did he need a coffee with his doughnuts?" Alex grinned.

Sue laughed as well then said, "I didn't see him with any white bakery bags, but he ordered a double espresso. He took it like a shot and then ordered a large black coffee to take with him while he toured the store."

Alex mused into her cup, "Is he still lurking around?"

Sue shrugged, drying her hands with a towel, "Not sure. Probably."

"Just because there's a detective roaming the aisles doesn't mean Sean was murdered. I mean, detectives investigate all kinds of deaths—even suicides to make sure there's no foul play. I'm sure this is just some routine follow-up thing."

It was Susan's turn to shrug before moving off to help the next customer who walked through the door.

Alex sipped the frothy goodness of her mocha, relishing the tendrils of warmth that curled around her insides, all the while pondering on what the presence of a detective might really mean.

Chapter 6

"Explain to me again why the cameras don't work," Detective Aubrey Steiner asked, trying to suppress the irritation from his voice. He was leaning forward, arms resting heavily on the sides of a rolling desk chair in the cramped office of the store manager—a rotund Caucasian male, nearing retirement, with sweat streaming from multiple parts of his body. And his deodorant was not doing a good enough job. Aubrey was starting to feel nauseous being in such close proximity to this man.

Nathan (Nate) Bartley took out a handkerchief and wiped away the sweat that was about to fall into his eyes. "Well, you see, the store was starting to fall behind budget wise, and I couldn't afford to keep them all turned on. Only the ones monitoring the set of front doors and the extremely expensive wines and liquors are still active. The others we kept as a sort of—what do you call it—an intimidation factor. Also, please call me Nate."

Nate's desk was cluttered with papers and an out of date computer that took up at least a third of surface space. There were also an array of family photos and knickknacks. On the walls hung a picture of the store's opening day with a 20 years younger version of Nate posing with hedge shears and a large red ribbon. There were also a couple of framed certificates and state licenses hanging from the walls, and one 5x7 of some poor kid stuffed into a Freddy the Ferret mascot costume, surrounded by a dozen or so kids during what looked like an in-store Easter egg hunt. Freddy's head was enormous with tiny black button eyes which reflected the flash so badly that in the picture they had turned red, and with a smile that was all teeth. . . but otherwise the walls in the office were bare.

Aubrey decided to change the subject and gestured to

the less creepy picture on the wall, "So you've been store manager since its christening? What year was that?"

"1995. I actually worked here before the Clivedales took over. It was just a Sentry back then, but with the take over I was promoted to store manager and have been ever since," Nate answered proudly. "I'll be retiring in about two years."

"And you know the owners pretty well then, yes?"

Nate nodded. "They're at their time share spot in Mexico right now—they're there for about half the year. My family spends Fourth of July at their barbeques almost every summer though!" Nate smiled at his boast, but quickly sobered when Aubrey's frown didn't waver. He added, "Of course they've been notified and have told me to cooperate in any way I can with the police. They're due to be back home in about two weeks or so."

"A man dies in their store and they don't fly back right away from their vacation?"

"Well, time shares aren't cheap and—"

Aubrey raised a hand to make the excuses stop. *What is this world coming to?* he thought to himself as he shifted to a more comfortable position, crossing one leg over the other and leaning back in the chair. Gesturing with his hands he said, "Mr. Bartley, I'm going to need to talk with some of your employees. Now I know that legally they do not have to talk to me unless they have a lawyer present, but I was hoping you wouldn't mind gathering everyone together shortly to explain to them the reason why I'm here. I'd like to urge anyone who might know or have seen anything suspicious to step forward. I was also hoping to use your office while I conduct these interviews. Maybe to make them feel more comfortable we could have you present in the room as well."

Nate paused before answering, "And all of this is just for a routine inspection you say? To tie up loose ends?"

Aubrey plastered a smile to his face as he said, "Of course Mr. Bartley. Any un-witnessed death needs to be inspected in such a manner. If this were indeed a murder investigation, no doubt the higher ups would get involved. They definitely wouldn't give this job to a rookie detective like me."

Mr. Bartley seemed to relax visibly at this declaration. It only made Aubrey's insides harden further. A mean voice somewhere deep within spoke up:

A rookie like me? I'm not a rookie by any means.

His more realistic self snapped back: *In the homicide division you are, boy, now get over it. Someone has to do the shitty jobs. You'll move up to real cases again soon enough.*

I've been doing investigations in general for three years already. . .

Do I have to remind you about what happened during the last big haul you tried to pull off by yourself? You're inexperienced, face it. Besides, you got the manager under your thumb just like you wanted, so shut up and focus!

Aubrey did as his sensible self said and shook his head to clear it. He and Nate left the office shortly after Nate made an announcement over the PA system that all available employees were to congregate to the atrium— a place where customers could sit and eat lunch if they wanted. Aubrey knew that he and the store manager would have to go to each department individually, in order to talk to the few who had to stay and man the fort while the others were in the impromptu meeting. This way, at least, most of them would be compiled into one location. Besides making his presence and objective known, Aubrey had another reason why he wanted Nate to gather everyone. He wanted to look each and every one of them in the eye.

As Mr. Bartley started his little speech, thanking the team for sticking together during this sad time. He carried on, making a few comments about what a good person and manager the deceased had been, etc., while Aubrey's gaze drifted across the sea of faces. There were about forty employees who worked at the grocery store, and about half were right there in front of him. Some were college kids, a few could be considered ancient, but the majority were all aged in between. And there were actually more women than men. He doubted that a woman would have the physical strength to push a grown, Navy-trained man down hard enough to crack his skull, and then drag and position his dead weight in the freezer. But Aubrey couldn't eliminate anyone just yet. He had done his homework during the few days when the store had been closed. He had read some interesting background checks and he wondered how well these people knew the people they were working next to.

Most kept their eyes trained to Mr. Bartley as he spoke, but tried sneaking peeks at Aubrey— the mysterious detective. He tried very hard not to laugh at how many times the eyes quickly darted away once they made contact with his own, like fish darting for cover once their bowl is tapped. Only a few people stared boldly at him—one being a mousy sort of looking girl who he guessed to be about his own age, maybe a little younger. He didn't care if he was being stared at. He was actually more interested to see how many of them refused to meet his gaze—a likely sign of guilt. There were a couple of those too which he mentally logged away to check into later.

Besides looking into their eyes to try and gain an initial perspective of those on his suspect list, he had a third reason for calling this meeting. By standing in front of everyone, he wanted to make himself "the talk of the town," so to speak. He knew that as soon as they walked away people would be discussing his presence and speculating about the body found in the freezer. He wanted the word to spread and the rumors to rise, allowing the random and seemingly insignificant details to surface so that when it did come time for him to talk to people, those thoughts would be in the forefront of their minds. He was hoping that the people might do his job for him and give him the leads he needed to follow, so that all he had to do was confirm everything as either truth or lie.

Alex was surprised when there was an announcement over the air phone sending everyone to the atrium. Her surprise was turned to understanding and then to curiosity as she realized why they had been called there—the detective was indeed in their midst and he was looking for information. She noted how he took the time to look at everyone around the room as if deciding which was the best cut of beef. When his eyes landed on hers she willed herself not to look away, but could feel her cheeks beginning to burn under his gaze. She was relieved he hadn't dallied on her face too long. Now *that* would have been embarrassing! Was he searching for a murderer? Did that mean that Sean's killer was among these people here?! Also, on a separate side note, he kind of looked familiar, didn't he? Then again he had the type of face that could blend into a crowd if it wanted to.

Alex's mind was moving in a multitude of directions as she went back to her department, but she wasn't able to ponder these things for long because the lunch rush started to hit. While serving up hot broasted chicken dinners, making sandwiches, and scooping cold salads, she tried to keep an eye on Nate and his companion as they went from department to department relaying the message for those who weren't able to attend the meeting in the atrium. She lost them for awhile, but noticed that the detective had finally ditched the store manager and had taken a seat in the atrium next to some of the regular lunch guests and began talking to them. She watched as the man's hard and intimidating persona melted away as he listened and then laughed with the people at his table. She couldn't hear what he was saying, but with this carefree attitude he seemed like a totally different person. Every once and awhile she noted how he scribbled something into a small notebook he kept open on the table.

"Jeez, you'd think with a dead person being found here, there would be less of a crowd."

Alex started at the sudden exclamation. Coming back to reality she turned to one of the college kids she worked with on the days he didn't have class. Brandon Nelson, the one who had spoken, was too tall and gangly to be compared to a leprechaun, but he did have the same colored hair, closely cropped, and a freckled face to go with it. She had nothing against him being a *ginger*, but when you added the fact that he was also left-handed, Alex couldn't help but laugh at the poor stereotypical fool. He was a good worker though, even with all of his inexperience (and complaints about working with kale), and Alex appreciated having him around to help.

She nodded at his remark and added, "I don't think we've ever been this busy on a non-holiday or non-sale day. But then, people are a lot more morbid then they give themselves credit for."

"True, dat!" Daniel, another co-worker who floated between deli and bagger work, confirmed from the other side of the salad case.

Alex walked around the prep table, and asked, "Did you need anything, Dan?"

"Yeah I'm on lunch. Give me a half pound of Taffy Apple salad. The fat kid inside me wants to come out." Alex rolled her eyes and began to dish out his "lunch." Daniel was a good kid, but he was definitely that—a kid. He supposedly turned really religious last year and joined a small Christian sect which he claimed had transformed his life. Now, even with his mock gangster talk and swagger, he wanted to go off to be a pastor (or whatever they called it), but everyone here was certain he was gay and couldn't wait to see how everything was going to play out.

"Anyways, I can't tell you how many times today I've been taking out people's groceries to their cars and been asked if I got to see *the body*? They keep asking for details, like if it was bloody, or if there was a break-in and honestly, I'm getting to the point where I want to start making things up. Maybe I'll get better tips that way."

"Well, good luck with that," Alex answered, giving him his fluff and hoping that would send him on his way.

"When I first got here that day, with all of those trucks, I wasn't sure what the heck was going on." Brandon chimed in.

Both Alex and Daniel turned toward Brandon, "That's right. You were supposed to be working that morning."

Brandon nodded. Alex thought back to her initial reaction to seeing all of the emergency vehicles and smiled, "That was an unnerving sight, although at first I thought maybe someone pulled another Stacy."

Daniel laughed, "Oh my gawd, I forgot about that!"

"Who's Stacy and what did she pull?" Brandon asked.

"That was just before you started working here. . . Stacy was a girl who used to work in bakery and she would always be the one to open the department."

"And as you know the bakery people have to be here at the un-godly hour of 4:30 to get the doughnuts and bread started," Daniel chimed in gleefully. He was a veteran like Alex, and he knew the outcome of this classic tale.

Alex continued, "For an hour or so each morning the bakery person is the only soul in the entire store, and on one morning Stacy accidently cut her finger. Apparently there was blood *everywhere*, like all over the floor and the prep table, and being all alone she panicked and called 911. Well the ambulance came and went and a few hours later she was back at work. Everyone was freaked out at first, wondering if she had lost a limb or something, but when she came back from the doctor's office, to everyone's dismay, she was perfectly fine—no stitches or anything. And a few days later she didn't even need a bandage."

"So of course the department heads were pissed," Daniel quickly picked up the thread, "because the store had to cover the cost of her idiocy. And now whenever someone nicks themselves, or even just gives themselves a paper cut the joke is: OH NO! I'm bleeding—better call 911!"

The three of them laughed together for a moment before they finally quieted down.

Daniel focused again on lunch, lifted the plastic container above his head to check the price on the bottom and said soberly, "But what's really sad about all this, it that

Sean's probably in Hell now."

"What?!" Alex and Brandon both exclaimed simultaneously.

"He told me recently that he turned Muslim. I told him that he needed to get off that path right away, otherwise its straight to Hell's doors, but he just laughed at me."

"Daniel you can't just go up to people and tell them they're going to Hell. That's just rude," Alex chided.

Daniel just threw up his hands and bounced away.

Alex walked back to where she had been attempting to make pistachio fluff (her all time favorite salad) to replace the Taffy Apple which was going to expire after today. She couldn't wait to try it once it was finished. "That kid is weird," she mumbled to herself as she picked up a spoon. She placed the spoon in the mixing bowl where the marshmallows and crushed pineapple lay inertly on top of the green pudding mix, but paused at the faint trickle of familiar chords playing over the speaker system. Craning her neck, she tried to figure out which song was starting. Normally she ignored whatever sappy love song spewed forth, but every once in awhile a catchy, upbeat one came on. Finally recognizing the quiet opening, she found herself smiling. *Here we go!* she thought to herself before opening her mouth and joining in:

I'm too hot—hot damn!

Been called a police and a fireman.

I'm too hot—hot damn!

Make a dragon wanna retire, man—

Brandon also found himself smiling because it wasn't

just Alex singing the pop song—the bakery and meat department people had joined in too. "I have to admit that I'm not much of a Bruno Mars fan, but this is probably the best song they play on this radio station that the store listens to."

"This one just doesn't get old," Alex agreed, her body slightly moving to the music. She didn't want to make too much of a fool out of herself (she knew she couldn't dance) but that didn't mean she wasn't allowed to have a little fun at work! Suddenly her peripheral vision picked up a familiar movement by the automatic entrance doors.

A young man about the age of twenty-six with a handsome movie star face and a toned body covered by a flawlessly tailored suit, overlapped by a trench coat to stall the cold, came gracefully toward the deli counter. Alex sighed as she thought to herself, *That boy doesn't just walk and he doesn't quite glide—he prances. And this blasted song is too damn perfect for him. Of* course *he comes in while it's playing. . .*

"Hey guys! Hi Alex! How's your day going?" The newcomer's voice was filled with genuine happiness just as his face was filled with a sort of peaceful and calming joy stemming from the beauty he found in everything around him. He was basically his own beacon in an otherwise cruel and hateful world. Alex was not only convinced that his light had a positive effect on everyone he came into contact with, but she was sure she had the biggest crush on this inspiring soul—a fact that scared her immensely considering she had sworn off love for the rest of eternity.

She tried to keep her voice neutral as she again walked over to the counter, "Hi Bobby, so you're working at the gentleman's clothing store again today, huh?" *He looks so fine in a suit!*

Bobby flashed his pearly whites, "Yes, just for a few hours. Listen, I taught this advanced yoga lesson this morning out by the lake." He leaned closer and his laughter sounded like the gentle pealing of bells as he admitted, "and I ended up falling in!"

Alex laughed also. *His imperfections just make him all the more perfect. Ugh! Did I just really think that?!* Mentally slapping herself she said, "I'm sorry, but that's hilarious. Did you need me to make you something today? Another Alex specialty—a Rabid Freddy Burger, perhaps?"

Bobby shook his head, "No I'm just running through today. Going to grab something premade, but I thought I'd just stop by and say hi." He turned to go then, raising a hand to wave as he called out from over his shoulder, "Have a good day!"

Alex gave the appropriate response and then walked back to her fluff which was still waiting to be mixed. Just seeing his face had elevated her heart rate, but it also made the small tear inside her heart hurt terribly. She mixed the ingredients in the bowl silently for a bit. Then after a while she paused, took a sampling spoon and scooped out a large glob for her own inspection. But the salad had turned bland, and she couldn't taste its sweetness.

It was about two o'clock when Alex noticed that the detective left. She hadn't seen him physically get up and leave, but when she looked over towards the atrium and found it completely empty. She felt disappointed, but wasn't exactly sure why. Maybe she had hoped something else exciting might have happened, like the murderer would pop out of hiding and try to take the detective out and there would be a shoot out and maybe even a hostage situation . . . but of course that type of thing generally only happened in the movies.

By this time in the afternoon the morning deli crew had also gone home, and now just Jacquelyn and herself were left to conquer the catering orders for the next day. There weren't that many, just a few fruit trays and one order of fifteen pounds of potato salad, so overall it was a quiet night. Spencer was due any minute to come and tame the savage mounds of dishes that harassed the sinks in back.

Jacquelyn (there were no nick names for her because at that moment there were three different Jack's that worked at the grocery store—Jacquelyn in Deli, Jackie was the store's florist, and Jack managed the produce department) peered closely at the strawberries before her before selecting the best looking ones to put on the catering trays. "These packs of berries remind me of playing Mine Sweeper—you pick up one of the pretty ones on top and all the others below it are moldy."

"Yeah, especially this time of year you need to be careful about that," Alex replied. There was a gargantuan metal bowl sitting in front of Alex, filled almost to the brim with the ingredients to make potato salad. All that was missing was the gallon of mayo. Unscrewing the lid to the mayonnaise container, Alex's mind shifted to a different train of thought. She had made this salad numerous times, but after working at the grocery store for awhile she had come to look upon this monstrous task a little differently.

Trying to bring her philosophical discovery to light she said, "You know, when I first started working here I felt this project to be never-ending. But now, I look at this bowl of starchy delights, which has to weigh at least twenty pounds, and realize that considering how much of this stuff we go through—it's really not that much."

"It still takes forever to make, in my opinion."

"Well, that's because you're kind of new. I feel like I've been working here forever."

"Two years isn't forever."

"You know what I mean. Anyways, do you think that change of thinking happens with other jobs? Like, if I was a sailor, would the ocean seem smaller after thirty years of sailing, or would it seem the same as the day I first boarded ship?"

"Only you would think of something like that. Just like when we had that pasta bar and you used to place the pesto, Alfredo, and tomato sauces in a specific order so that they matched Italy's flag, remember that?"

"I never said I was normal."

"True. Moving on to more grounded topics. . . Detective Aubrey Steiner," drawled Jacquelyn as she plopped a heap of sliced strawberries on the center of each tray, "now he's a looker. His eyes are really green—did you get a good look at them? Like emeralds! And he looked to be about your age too. You should try and date him."

Alex laughed and rolled her eyes, "Stop it, Jacquelyn! Why do you think I need to date someone anyways? Just this week alone you mentioned Bobby, Jake, Ginger Brandon and even the old guy in meat department!"

"Frank isn't that old and you two talk a lot."

"Yes, I talk a lot with lots of people and about all sorts of subjects. Just because I talk to people doesn't mean I want to date them."

"But—"

"Stop. Just stop."

There was a moments silence while the two girls worked on their respective projects.

Then Alex asked playfully, "Why don't you try to date him? You're single too, right? And he seems older than me. Closer to your age."

Both of the girls jumped as Spencer spoke from behind them. He was just arriving and putting his stuff in the designated area for employee coats and things when he said, "Are you talking about that cop? He's twenty-seven."

"And how in the world do you know that?" Alex snapped, irked by the way this kid had a habit of sneaking up on her.

Spencer shrugged, "I'm just good with telling people's ages. He said hi to me on his way out, introduced himself. So Sean was really murdered then."

"We don't actually know yet. They're 'still investigating.' "

Spencer turned to go into the back where he was most likely going to play some upbeat, but obscene music from his iPod and then start cracking down on some grease and grime when Alex stopped him, "Hey, wait. How old am I?"

Spencer pondered a moment then stated, "Twenty-five. She's thirty-one." Then without waiting for a response, he went into the kitchen.

"That kids good," Jacquelyn whistled.

"He was dead on," Alex added. The girls paused at the bad choice of words and then burst out laughing. Morbid humor is sometimes the best kind.

Their laughter was put on pause when the department phone started ringing. Alex picked it up on the second ring and gave the standard greeting, "Forestgrove Grocery, this is Alex speaking. How may I help you?"

A familiar voice responded, "Ah, hello Alex. This is Mai. I wasn't sure who to call, but on Nate's schedule he has me opening the deli tomorrow and I don't think I will be able to make it in. . ."

Alex frowned, "Are you sick? That's no good, but then again it is that time of year, right?"

There was an awkward pause from the other end and then hesitantly Mai said, "Actually I'm not sick. It's just that, well, there's already one ghost that lives between those walls, and now with Sean's death—"

Alex cut her off, "Mai there are no such things as ghosts. I've worked all day today and haven't seen the slightest sign of one. I promise, you'll be fine."

Alex was the first person to befriend Mai when she started working in the deli a few months back. Mai was older than Alex, somewhere in her forties. She was of Asian descent and very shy. She was also very superstitious. About a month into her job, Mai had stumbled onto the knowledge that someone had died in the grocery store some seven or so years before.

The lady who passed away could have been straight off the boat from Germany, with a thick accent, who worked the meat counter. Then one day she walked into Receiving, claimed to a passerby that she felt like her insides were shutting down, and had a heart attack and died only a few moments later.

Ever since then, on early mornings or late nights

when not too many people are about, strange things were said to occur—running footsteps heard moving down empty aisles, random clapping noises, whispered names, and loaves of bread knocked down from their shelves. Whenever something weird might happen, veteran grocery workers would often say, "Oh, it's the bread ghost again, hard at work!" But Alex didn't believe in such nonsense, and actually found it irritating that Mai was using this new death as an excuse to back out of her responsibilities.

"I'm sorry Alex, but my horoscope says to be weary of the supernatural auras this month. And I think you should take care as well. We share the same birth month, you know."

"Mai—"

"Goodbye Alex. I wish you luck and good fortune."

And with that final utterance, Mai hung up.

Alex held the phone up to her ear for a second longer before placing it gently back into its cradle. Sighing, she then dug through the binders placed beside the phone, looking for the employee number listings buried there. When she found the list she picked up the phone again and reluctantly dialed a number. *Claire isn't going to like having to open again tomorrow, but there's no one else to call, and she* is *the temporary head of the department.* When a sleepy sounding Claire answered, Alex quickly relayed the sad news, leaving out the part about ghosts.

For Alex, the only other highlight of the work night was when she was leaving. She paused at the courtesy desk to say hello to Tim, another one of her closer co-workers.

Tim was busy counting the deposits for the night so he didn't answer right away. Alex leaned against the counter, her eyes wandering over the numerous lottery scratch offs.

"It's Alex!" he said as he set down the green and somewhat crumpled bills.

"How are things with you? How's Megan?"

"Oh, you know, living the dream. Working. Paying bills. Planning a wedding. We sent out the Save the Dates yesterday. You should be getting yours soon."

"Alright, I'll keep an eye out." With a lowered voice she asked, "So what do you think about this Sean thing? You think it was a murder?"

Tim scoffed rather loudly, "The guy was too much of a jerk to die any other way." Then quietly he added, "And something else happened here around that time too—something bad enough it's got Julie smoking again. The store's big safe was short $500."

"What! Are you serious?"

Tim's breast puffed up as he said, "See no one noticed until I counted it on the 31st for inventory purposes. People are supposed to count it every night, but they don't. And I had the day before that off, so it had to have happened the day before or the day of Sean's murder."

"Who all has access to that stuff?"

"Well, me of course, Julie, and Nate, but the keys stay up here during our breaks. So basically anyone could have taken it."

"Holy crap. Do you really think it's all connected?"

Tim nodded, "Yep, and tomorrow when that detective guy shows up I'm going to tell him about it. It might help close this case."

Chapter 7

After Aubrey left the grocery store around two in the afternoon, he made his way back to the precinct to work on some paperwork. In his Dodge Ram truck it was about a fifteen minute drive between these two destinations, only another seven minutes from the police station to his apartment, and during those twenty-two minutes Aubrey was almost assaulted twice by stupid drivers going too fast for the slippery conditions. He couldn't wait for spring—better yet, summer—when all of this dirty mush that clogged the roads disappeared, the winds were warm and fair again, and he could pull his 2005 black Pontiac GTO out of storage and cruise the streets with a bit more style. He preferred his GTO more for sentimental reasons, but knew that it made a terrible winter car and so every November, sometimes October, he said goodbye to his little car, and greeted his bulky but dependable muscle truck that could roll over snow banks with only minor difficulty, depending on their height.

Most people thought winter was supposed to be on its way out by February, but Wisconsinites knew differently. January, February, and March could still do the same tricks as a late December month—sometimes even worse. Back in March, 2011, Wisconsin had its largest storm in over 120 years, the third largest in the state's history. A low pressure system clashed with a pocket of cold air, leading to sleet and freezing rain, and ended with a pile up of 17.8 inches of snow in Green Bay, and a two thousand foot media tower knocked over in Eau Claire. Yes, winter didn't like to make things easy here in the Cheese State, and it didn't like to release its hold either.

There was supposedly another ice storm headed Sheboygan's way in the next two days and if it hit as hard as it was doing in the neighboring states, then chaos would ensue, maybe even breaking the 2011 record. There would be power outages, frozen pipes, broken furnaces and a multitude of cops and technicians called to duty to try and deal with the mess. . .

What a wonderful time to celebrate Valentine's Day, no?

Luckily for Aubrey, he didn't have any plans for Valentine's Day—either on the weekend right before or on the actual Monday that it fell on—so he was free to heed emergency calls if needed. Personally though, Valentine's Day had always seemed like a stupid holiday to him—one that only helps the greeting card companies, and he hated how it made him feel obligated to buy a girl something when he didn't really like her the way his Valentine Card told her he did.

Being honest, his loathing toward lovey-dovey holidays might have to do with the fact that his last serious relationship was when he was still in high school—a fact which made Aubrey blush every time he thought about it. Of course he had dated a few girls here and there, but college and the Police Academy had taken the majority of his time and focus. He also didn't believe in frivolous love and decided that once he was where he wanted to be with his career, then he could take some time to find "the one."

Besides, he really could use the over time. He needed to start saving more of his dough too. The apartment he lived in was okay, the second story of a house that had seen better days with peeling paint and a slanted front porch. His accommodations included two bedrooms, his own kitchen and bathroom. But cold air leaked crazily in through the old windows and his heating bill this year had been steep. There were also cracks in the walls and the little balcony he had was probably a safety hazard. But it was his place, his refuge from the cruelties he had to face every day, and for now it would do.

When Aubrey entered his apartment he took off his coat and threw it over the back of one of the three mismatched dining room chairs he had surrounding a card table and walked over to the fridge. It was completely empty except for a bottle of ketchup, a jar of pickles, and an opened twenty-four pack of Miller—bottles, not cans. There was a difference in taste depending which container you drank the concoction out of, and Aubrey preferred the pure hoppy taste the glass gave as opposed to the metallic one an aluminum can provided.

Aubrey was about to grab for one of the bottles to start his unwinding process when the landline phone that came with the apartment started to ring. Only a few people knew that number existed so he let it ring until the answering machine picked it up. Aubrey selected a bottle and popped the cap while he waited.

When the machine finally kicked in a rough, male voice spoke tentatively though the speakers of the box, "Hey Aubrey, just calling to say hi. Me and your mother haven't heard from you for a while, and while I was playing cards with the boys they told me how you're on a new case. . . I'm happy to hear you're back on the horse, so to speak. . . I mean after that last incident, well you know, I just want you to know I'm happy that you're sticking with it. Police work is good work and I know in time you'll. . ." Aubrey took a large swig of the beer, his face set in a frown as he continued to listen to the message. "Aww, heck, just give us a call, okay? And if you need any help with your case you can always talk to me. I was a detective for nearly twenty years before I got shot and then had to retire. . . Just call, anytime. We'll be here."

Aubrey glared at the little blinking light on the

answering machine for a minute before hitting the delete button. He finished his beer in one long, final inhale and went back to the fridge seeking more.

Chapter 8

It was nearing three o'clock in the afternoon the next day when Aubrey found himself alone in the manager's office with his hands running through his hair, his eyes trying to bore holes into the case notes sitting before him, hoping that some epiphany might present itself.

Out of the forty-six employees here at Forestgrove Grocery, only a handful actually had the muscle strength to take out an ex-navy man, let alone drag an unconscious body to a freezer and position it the way it was found—that is, if that really was what happened. So far the only evidence of foul play was that damned perimortem bump on the dead man's head and for all he knew maybe the guy was a klutz, ran into something and then stumbled to the freezer—maybe to finish up inventory since it was the end of the month—and then got dizzy, sat down to rest, and ended up falling asleep as a result of a concussion. But his gut instincts were churning like crazy on this one. Something was off, and he just needed to figure out what.

What was really missing from this case was motive.

His interviews had actually started a few days before the grocery store had re-opened, the first one conducted at the home of the deceased.

Mrs. Edith Ritter was in her early thirties, but the death of her husband seemed to age her another ten years. The strain of having to raise two young children on her own was settling into a harsh reality and future. She claimed to really miss her husband, but as she talked Aubrey noted a thin layer of anger or maybe even jealousy behind the words, as if she thought he had died on purpose.

No, Sean didn't have any enemies. He only had admirers. He worked all the time, most of the time not making it home until midnight or later. He was also going to school to gain a Master's in Business Administration at the local college. Every other day or so he hung out with some of his old Navy buddies. End of interview.

Aubrey had followed the Navy buddy angle and tracked down the guy's closest two pals in a local rat-infested hell hole where the beer was cheap and the girls were fully endowed. Three drinks and a litany of shared police force/military training stories and jokes later, Aubrey came away with a fact that he was sure Mrs. Ritter didn't know, or else she had neglected to pass along to him at their first meeting. It seemed Mr. Ritter had a thing for the younger ladies and had even been charged the year before with sexual harassment in the work place. That's what really turned Aubrey's attention to the employees of Forestgrove Grocery. Freddy the Ferret had always seemed a little too cute (or in the case of the large mascot costume, very creepy) and Aubrey was sure that behind those beady little eyes, there were storage areas full of skeletons.

Going through background checks of the employees there, Aubrey was amused by how many of these innocent looking people had rap sheets and ties to the law. Possession of multiple kinds of drugs, theft, attempted robbery, and even assault charges—it was all here, tucked between the aisles of white bread and soup cans. And he had had a busy morning trying to talk to as many of these interesting people as possible.

He started his day by speaking with the flower lady. He knew she didn't have the body strength to take out a grown man; she was late fifties, frail, and gentle looking. But her daughter had been sexually assaulted during her high school years, so if anyone would have a vendetta against a potential sexual predator, Aubrey figured that Jackie would be at the top of the list.

So around seven in the morning of February 11th, Aubrey strolled into the floral department where suspected accomplice (if nothing else) #1 was busily arranging a bouquet of red roses and baby's breath in a heart-shaped vase.

"Good morning, ma'am. My name is Detective Steiner. I bet you're busy trying to catch up on orders, after all it is almost Valentine's Day. Would I be bothering you if I asked you a few questions?"

Jackie gave him the once-over, then turned her nervous eyes back to her project. "With the 'accident' and the store being shut down, it has pushed me behind, but no, I don't mind answering a few questions."

The floral department was small, with a multi-leveled tier displaying a variety of houseplants and teddy bears in front, a cooler holding artfully completed flower arrangements to the right, and a work space that took up the rest of the area. While Aubrey asked his few basic introductory questions he walked around the cramped space, glancing at the various shelves containing ribbons, bows, and vases of varying sizes. He paused at the counter next to Jackie where a few archaic and dangerous looking tools all sat in an organized row. They were all pained a sickly green color and the visible blades were flecked with rust.

"What are these for?" He asked, the perplexity clear on his face. "This one looks like a guillotine for fingers. . ."

Jackie chucked, "For flowers, yes. It trims off the ends very nicely."

"And this one looks like something that might rip off

finger nails. . ."

"Not quite." Jackie took a fake flower from a random drawer and placed the stem in a hole that was just big enough for a thumb to fit. There was a metallic grinding noise, and when she pulled the stem out Aubrey was surprised to see a sharpened metal barb on the fake flower's end. Jackie stabbed the barb into a square of green Styrofoam and went back to fixing her rose arrangement.

If this lady snapped, I don't think she'd let the person just freeze to death. I think she'd torture the poor soul first! Aubrey swallowed away the mental images of severed fingers and pressed on to more specific questions. "It was rumored that Sean was popular with the young ladies here. Did you notice any specific ones that he was, shall we say, partial to?"

Jackie paused for just a beat before finishing the bow she was making and turned to add the finished piece to its brothers and sisters in the flower cooler. "He was hanging around the bakery girls all the time. One rarely saw Sean working out front because he believed menial jobs were beneath him—but he often helped out the girls in bakery. He tried hitting on one of the grocery girls from up front too, her name was Kristy, but she was already Parker's pet at the time. The boys had some sort of scuffle about it."

Aubrey checked his notes, "Parker, the grocery manager? You mean he was dating one of his underlings?"

Jackie's eyes shifted around as if making sure no one else was listening. "Well, not officially. It's against company policy for managers to date their subordinates."

"So they were trying to keep it a secret?"

Jackie nodded. She started to pull out supplies for her

next project as she explained, "It was a secret until Sean found them stealing kisses outside one day. Kristy quit before they could fire her. Parker was angry for quite awhile about it."

"Thank you Jackie, you've been a great help. If you can think of anything else, here's my card. Oh, and Jackie—you do wonderful work. My aunt used to run a flower shop and I helped her out once and awhile when I was younger, but your work blows hers right out of the water. If I had someone worth giving flowers to, I'd definitely give her one of your creations."

Jackie blushed as she thanked him. Then she took a stray yellow bloom from a water bucket on the floor, clipped it close to the petals and before he could protest she slipped it through the button hole on one of his breast pockets of his over coat. "I'll keep my ears open. Sean wasn't the best fellow around, but he didn't deserve to be killed and then left in a freezer—if that is what happened." She shivered visibly with the thought.

It was Aubrey's turn to thank her, which he did with real sincerity before moving on to talk with his next suspect.

Parker Loid had been one of the names at the top of his list. He was young, 29 to be exact, and obviously fit by the way he carried large crates of dry goods without showing any signs of difficulty. He had also been busted for possession of marijuana twice so far, the last bust being two and a half years prior. Aubrey had originally speculated that Sean somehow found out about his co-worker's drug dealings and maybe tried to blackmail him, but now, with the tip about his girlfriend, maybe Parker had two reasons to get rid of Sean.

Aubrey found the guy out back taking a smoke break.

Even with the brisk air, he stood coatless with legs apart, back straight, one hand resting on his hip, with his shirt sleeves rolled to the elbows showing off a multitude of tattoos, and black hair reflecting the winter sun atop his scalp. *God, if he had blond hair he would look exactly like a young Robert Redford*, Aubrey mused to himself.

When the back door opened, Parker turned and frowned as he discovered that Aubrey was the one stepping though.

"Got a spare you can borrow me?"

"Sure do, partner," Parker responded politely enough as he dug into a pants pocket and took out a crumpled pack of Marlboro Reds.

"Got a light to go with it?"

Parker gave a low, very guttural laugh that definitely marked the guy as a stoner before saying, "Never leave without one."

After lighting up the two smoked in silence for a while. Finally Aubrey broke the ice, "Haven't had one of these in a while."

"Yeah?"

"Haven't had a lot of stuff in a while—not since college, man. Me and my buddies used to get fucked up real good." Aubrey thought his hint was obvious, but Parker didn't bite.

Instead, Parker finished his cigarette and tossed it into the butt barrel. He was just passing Aubrey to go back inside when Aubrey spoke up again, "A little bumblebee told me that the dead guy in the freezer caught you making out with a fellow employee back by these dumpsters."

"Oh, yeah? And what does that have to do with anything?"

Aubrey took a final drag, dropped the end on the ground and crushed it beneath a shoe. He ignored Parker's question and asked instead, "Bet that pissed you off, huh?"

"That prick didn't see anything. Sean made all that shit up about me just because Kristy wouldn't give him the time of day. The guy was a creep and a fucking liar!"

"So are you still seeing Kristy or is it no longer fun because you can't fool around in the work place?"

Aubrey couldn't help but smirk as he watched Parker's hands ball into fists. Sometimes gestures spoke louder than verbal communication and this was such a time.

"We weren't stupid enough to do things here at work."

"But you and Sean did fight about it. Did it come to fists? Or just words?"

"He deserved to get his ass beat, but no, I never hit him. Now excuse me, but I have shelves to stock."

Well, he didn't deny anything. If he did murder the coordinator, would he have held his tongue better? Or is his mind fried from too many drugs, and he's too stupid to keep the details to himself?

Aubrey checked his watch and saw that it was only eight in the morning. He had been too nauseous to eat anything before, but now his stomach felt as hollow as a cave come night time when all of its winged occupants have left. He decided to order breakfast from the deli and scope out the crew there.

Claire Debauch, the lady who had found the body, was working. He had already talked to her on that "fun" Monday when the incident was still fresh on her mind. She had been quite distraught, but then any normal person would be. Aubrey was pretty sure her hysteria had been genuine and that she herself wasn't the killer. From talking with Nate about the managerial structure of the place, he had learned that Mrs. Debauch would have been the next in line for authority in the deli department, previously only answering to Sean or Nate the Great. Apparently Nate had offered Claire the deli/bakery coordinator position after Sean's death, but she had refused, saying something about too much stress or something. It could be a ploy to draw away unwanted attention, but his gut instincts didn't warrant Mrs. Debauch as any sort of threat.

Aubrey glanced at the giant chalk board nailed to the wall behind the deli counter which had the kitchen's menu written on it. On one side was written the lunch menu, and the other listed breakfast items. Even with his stomach set on morning delights, he took the time to read through the lunch options, just in case he would be sticking around that long. There were eight different hot sandwiches that you could order, and Aubrey was momentarily disappointed that there was no Pastrami on Rye.

Some deli this is, he thought to himself and then shrugged. *At least they can make Rueben's. I guess that's kind of close. . .*

With his mind made up Aubrey placed his order with a different deli girl, someone who had been hired the week before her manager had died. She smiled sweetly as he sauntered over and barely took her eyes off of him the entire time he was ordering. He didn't mind the attention but prayed that she had recorded everything correctly. He was very particular on how he liked his eggs.

While he waited he watched the people behind the counters. The bakery and the deli departments were connected and separated from the selling floor by a snaking case of glass that was divided by a hot case that was currently empty, but he assumed would soon be filed with chicken, fries, and other deep fried treats that made up the American diet.

There were three young women working in the deli. One was making cold, grab and go sandwiches, another was working on stocking items on the mini salad bar, and the third, Claire, seemed to be compiling catering orders of some kind. A fourth girl pushed through the receiving doors and hurried over, checking over the finished catering parcels before snagging a handful and rushing back the way she had come. She was one of the delivery drivers no doubt, and for an instant Aubrey got the mental image of Sean as the deli pimp.

He laughed to himself as he strolled past the empty hot case and over to the bakery side. Doughnuts of all sorts greeted his eyes along with muffins, freshly baked bagels, and croissants. At his approach the single girl behind the counter came forward and asked if he needed anything. She too was a cute looking one, he guessed her age to be about twenty-seven like him. She hadn't been one of the ones on his list that he originally wanted to seek out to talk to, but he had time to kill.

Besides, she brought up the subject first by asking, "Hey, aren't you that detective that's been hanging around? Find out anything interesting?"

Aubrey decided to play it coy, "Oh, just a few little things. Does that chocolate Long John have Fritos on it? I've never seen something like that before." He was bent over looking at the case and before standing up he glanced at her name tag. Apparently her name was Cyndi. Seeing her name sparked the realization that she was one of the ones working the night Sean kicked the bucket.

"Yeah, we have some pretty crazy things here," she said, her smile displaying her even, white teeth.

"Say, were you working the night that, you know. . ." Aubrey didn't want to frighten this doe away from the topic. The girl nodded so he asked, "Was Sean out here at all that day? Was he acting strange?"

He was surprised when she produced an eye roll, "He was always out here. It was kind of annoying, actually. He knew I was seeing someone, but I wouldn't tell him who it was and so Sean was constantly bugging me about it. The bakery usually closes at six, but with him around I got so far behind that I was here until almost store close."

"That must have been really annoying. Did Sean know the guy? Is that why you didn't want to tell him who it was?"

Aubrey had thought he had asked this last round of questions quite casually, but Cyndi instantly clammed up after they were asked.

She laughed and then winked at him, "Oh you don't want to hear about my love life. It's not that great anyways. But if you need something sugary just let me know!"

As she turned to go back to whatever she had been doing before, Aubrey heard the call of "Order Up!" and went to go retrieve his morning meal.

Chapter 9

Aubrey was greatly disappointed in his breakfast. The bacon wasn't crisp enough, he felt they had skimped on the potatoes, and his eggs were runny in the middle. He hated runny eggs. Sighing, he picked up his plate and reluctantly headed back to the deli counter. He hated being that person, but runny eggs he could not tolerate.

The same girl that helped him before, apologizing, took his plate back into the kitchen. There was a loud clanging as if something had been thrown half way across the room, a slew of curse words, and the deli girl quickly scuttled from the kitchen. She said it would be out momentarily.

Aubrey's brows were knit together and his arms folded across his chest when three minutes later the chef himself appeared from the kitchen and handed Aubrey his plate of breakfast. "You had the 'fried hard' eggs, sir?" he asked, but Aubrey and probably the rest of the world could easily see through that façade of civility.

"I did. And I'm sorry, but I can't stand having runny eggs. I also don't like scrambled. That's why I ordered them 'fried hard.' "

The chef was an older gentleman with a slight limp in his step and salt and pepper hair all over his head. He also had the stubbornness of a mule. "I've been making eggs for near thirty years now, professionally, and that's how 'fried hard' eggs come about. Now if the order sheet had read 'break the yolk' I would have understood better."

"Alright, next time I'll ask for them broken, as well as smashed with a hammer, held firmly against the grill till they're screaming, and then reawakened with a lil' bourbon, a teaspoon of Tobasco, and a mass of salt. How's that sound?"

The chef blinked a couple of times before letting out a belly-giggling laugh that made everyone in the area turn to look in their direction. Aubrey guessed this old coot didn't laugh too often. "And next time I'd like a few more potatoes."

"Need to soak up a few litters, eh? I can get you more potatoes. See that's how Mr. Ritter made me ration them out, but he's gone and dead now, so I suppose I can go back to the old way I used to be cooking—back when things tasted like they should!" The old man held out his hand. It was callused all over the palm, and had a healing burn on the top. "Name's Larry Duke. What's yours lad?"

Aubrey took the offered hand and endured the viselike grip, "Detective Aubrey Steiner, at your service, sir."

"Ah, a public defender. And they gave you the crappy job of trying to figure out who killed that idiot, book-learning scoundrel, eh?"

"Unfortunately, yes they did."

Larry leaned closer, patted Aubrey's arm sympathetically, and said, "Well, that guy was an asshole."

"I've been hearing something along those lines."

"I wouldn't be surprised if lots of people wanted to have him offed. He kept going around like he owned the place, and saying that if he weren't here we would all be lost or something. Well, he's gone now and the store is still turning without him. Ha! Wish he were alive just so I could stick him with that!"

"Did you ever see Sean being extra friendly to any of the ladies that work here?"

Larry scoffed. Leaning even closer he whispered,

"Most of these girls aren't really ladies. More like unpaid whores." He winked as he added in a louder voice, "Now you enjoy that plate there. Next time I'll fix you up something on the house."

Aubrey thanked him and went back to his table, deep in thought.

After that his day went by quickly. He used the passwords that Nate gave him to take a gander at the deceased's emails and documents on his work computer located in bum-fuck-Egypt (a.k.a. the random back alley of the store). He printed out about thirty or so e-mails to go through later at leisure. He rifled through the guy's desk even though forensics had already done a thorough job, glanced at the scant two personal photos of family, played with Sean's stress ball, and laughed at the cartoon cadaver which had the dual purpose of paper weight and pen holder. How ironic that the dead guy owned a "dead guy."

He also talked to a few more people.

He talked to Daniel Pertz, the bagger who was one of the two who had closed the store that night. The kid had just turned 18, was finally able to use the box crusher as well as scan alcohol, and he seemed extremely proud of himself. He was also a religious nut. Surprising, considering the long rap sheet Aubrey had skimmed through.

Possession of multiple kinds of drugs, under aged drinking, and one account of attempted robbery were at the top of the list. Aubrey felt sorry for the kid because of the home problems he came from, but changed his mind when the religious talk started. Daniel didn't show any remorse about the dead coordinator. Said he deserved it for turning Muslim (which had to have been a baited trick because according to Sean's wife they were both Lutherans). Said that

God knows what's in our hearts and will punish the wicked. When Aubrey asked if Sean and Daniel had ever had issues about anything the kid had answered that yes, they had. Sean got mad at Daniel when he said that he couldn't work on Sundays anymore in the deli, and that Sean teased him when he refused to sell people Beer Cheese Dip because alcohol is against his religion.

"Strange that someone who used to binge drink every weekend and even tried to steal from a liquor store should now condemn others for wanting a little taste of fermentation with their pretzels," Aubrey had remarked snidely.

Daniel had turned red and replied hotly, "That was before I turned to God! I'm a changed man now!"

"I can tell," was Aubrey's terse response before sending the Christian on his way.

He also talked to the store's one and only man of color who worked there whose only response was, "You think I killed him because I'm black, right?" Aubrey noted that guy had only worked there for two and a half weeks before the death occurred, decided that he need not make a further inquiry, and quickly walked away from that one.

After that Aubrey had made a few phone calls while eating his lunch (the Rueben he had spied on the deli menu earlier, which was extremely well made) in Mr. Bartley's office. He called the cleaning company and discovered they only come in every other night to wash and wax the floors and that January 31st had been their off day. He called the few employees who had quit because of the death in the hopes of maybe meeting them face to face, none of whom agreed and gave "no comment" remarks like he was a reporter or something. He also called HQ to see if they had found any previous records of sexual harassment charges for the deceased. None had turned up. Apparently the incident that the navy buddies gloated about hadn't pressed any charges.

He was just putting his cell phone away when there was a knock on the office door and another one of the suspects near the top of the list poked his head through. His name was Timothy Marks, which he offered freely along with a hand to be shaken, and eagerly took a seat across from the detective, claiming that he didn't need Nate's extra presence. Tim was maybe twenty-five, but had a young look about him with gray eyes and wavy brown hair. He was out of uniform, Aubrey observed, making him wonder if this was the guy's day off.

Tim started right to the point, which was fine for Aubrey. Excitedly he said, "I discovered an unusual occurrence the night Mr. Ritter passed while I was closing the store and I figured you would want to know right away. The safe out front was short $500 and it had to have been taken sometime during the day before, or the morning of the murder. I believe this is either a blackmailing case or a petty theft gone wrong. If you want my opinion. . ."

While he was speaking in his homily way, Aubrey was trying to figure out what this guy reminded him of with his head held extra high and his chest puffed out in grandeur. This guy figured he had found the holy grail of the mystery, the missing piece of the puzzle! Too bad the missing money had already been reported at the beginning of the investigation. It was one more question he hadn't yet found an answer to.

"A peacock!" Aubrey said under his breath, finally figuring out what this guy looked like.

Tim stopped talking at this strange remark and asked,

"What?" rather lamely.

Aubrey just waved his revelation away and asked instead, "I heard you're getting married in a few months. Congratulations." Tim beamed and would have started talking again if Aubrey hadn't quickly intervened, "Weddings sure do cost a lot, huh? And you with a grocery-man's salary. . . Ah, but you're from Chicago-land right? I bet your parents can cover the costs. Or do mommy and daddy not help out that much?"

"What are you getting at?" Tim asked coldly. "Are you trying to say that *I* stole that money?"

Aubrey shrugged, "Weddings are expensive. And you did close the store the night Sean was murdered. Maybe he saw you taking the money and was going to turn you in so you bashed him in the head and dragged him to the freezer—"

"This is ridiculous! I'm a suspect!? I'm trying to help you, you fuck—"

"Careful. You wouldn't want to offend an officer of the law, now would you?"

Tim shut his mouth, his whole body quivering and seething with rage while Aubrey imagined feathers slowly deflating. Or would they be flared in anger?

"Anything else you'd like to add?" Aubrey asked calmly. He was enjoying this.

"Not without a lawyer present!" Tim snapped, standing and walking away with as much dignity as he could muster before slamming the door behind him.

With the door closed, Aubrey let out a little laugh. Taunting him had been fun. He didn't actually think Tim had stolen anything. The peacock's pride was way too big for something like that. However, that didn't mean he was off the suspect list.

It was now 3:15 p.m. Of his list of possible suspects only about half of the people he wanted to talk to were crossed off. After finding out that Jack, the produce department head, was in a wheel chair, Aubrey was able to eliminate him as a suspect. But there was still Evan, from the meat department to check up on. He was one of the ones keeping his eyes down during Nate's speech the day before. *And I should probably talk to the peacock's boss as well as consult the head liquor guy—find out if Sean liked his wine red or white,* Aubrey chuckled to himself.

He then gave out a long sigh, rubbing his fingers against his eyes. He could feel a thirst for a beer coming on, and for the most part his interviews could wait until tomorrow, but he still had one more person he wanted to talk to before heading out for the day.

Chapter 10

Alex started the day of February 11th later then planned due to an alarm which never went off, so she wasn't able to make much use of the Wi-Fi at the coffee shop before she started her shift at Forestgrove Grocery. The arrival of the detective yesterday had piqued her interest and because she wanted to learn more about him, she found herself in Capital E. Chino's during her half hour lunch break.

The coffee shop had been really busy in the morning, but now around 3 o'clock it was completely empty. Sipping a small coffee at one of the window tables, Alex read aloud what little of Steiner's bio she could find to Susan who leaned lazily upon the counter.

"Detective Aubrey Steiner of the Sheboygan Police Department graduated from Lakeland College in 2009 with a double major in Criminal Justice and Sociology as well as a minor in Police Science with an added emphasis in forensic study. He then went on to graduate at the top of his class at the Police Academy, and started employment with Milwaukee's undercover Narcotic's Unit in 2012. He transferred back to his hometown in October of last year, 2014, after obtaining the rank of detective. You can contact Detective Steiner by calling the Sheboygan Police Department, extension. . ."

"Nothing else?" Susan asked. "So he's not married? Find out if he has a Facebook page so we can see if he has a girlfriend—better yet, Google him so we can see if he turns up on any newsfeeds!"

Alex rolled her eyes, "I already checked. He doesn't have a Facebook page and the only couple of things that turn up on Google are his biography from the Police Department's page and a few news articles about some major drug bust that he was a part of in Milwaukee last year. Nothing else. I think he's too new at being a cop to have his name all over the place."

Susan nodded, "I wonder why he moved back to Sheboygan. Nothing ever happens here."

It was Alex's turn to nod her head in understanding, "Sheboygan is like a black hole. Nothing really goes on here except drinking, and yet so many tourists are drawn here. Did you know that there's a large surfing crowd that comes every year to Sheboygan and stays at Blue Harbor—that resort right on Lake Michigan? Not to mention all of the Japanese and European vacationers who come to stay at The American Club and then find their way into the back streets of Sheboygan-town. What's really weird, is that most of the people I know who currently live here weren't even born here! They're from Chicago, or Indiana, or even from the east coast and yet they moved *here* of all places! At least Detective Steiner has some excuse. At least he was born around here."

"Oh! I almost forgot! Jennifer worked this morning. Apparently Detective Steiner stopped in again and he ordered the same thing as yesterday: a double espresso which he downed right on the spot and then a coffee to go."

"He either really likes coffee or he doesn't sleep much," Alex mused.

"Or maybe his Sheboygan heritage is sticking out," Sue pointed out, a twisted grin on her face.

Their conversation was halted by the abrupt entrance of an upset Tim who, once he noticed Alex and Susan sitting by themselves in the coffee shop through the windows, stormed his way inside with a sudden need to vent his frustrations.

"That detective guy is a serious douchebag! Hi Sue, give me a large caramel macchiato, skim milk, with an extra shot of espresso!"

Susan and Alex made eye contact before Susan went off to fill his order.

"Uh, hi Tim. I take it you talked to Detective Steiner like you were planning on, huh?" Alex asked hesitantly. She knew Tim well enough to know that you had to be cautious when approaching him while he was so riled up.

He turned on her almost savagely as he slammed some bills down on the counter to pay for his drink, "Yes I did and that bastard didn't even thank me for coming forward. And the best part? The best part is that I'm a suspect! Me! I mean seriously, what a dunce! Listen, do NOT talk to that guy without a lawyer! I don't plan to ever again, and in fact, when I get home I'm going to call my lawyer and get that guy suspended for badgering and false accusations!"

Alex gave a sympathetic shake of her head, when really she was thinking, *Well of course you're a suspect. You were one of the last people to probably see Sean alive and you are one of the only people with access to the safe. And calling your lawyer in such a situation? You were the one who offered to talk to the guy without a witness present. There's nothing your lawyer can do for you except charge you for a consultation.* Those years of watching *Judge Judy* and *Law and Order* with her mom were finally paying off.

Instead of revealing what she was thinking she said instead, "If it makes you feel better, I'm probably one of his suspects also. I was one of the last people to see Sean alive. In fact, I got out so late that night that I think you made your rounds before I left my department, right? So that means I talked to the victim after you did. I also left after you, so unless you came back and murdered him—"

"That's preposterous! Of course I didn't—"

"I like your use of the term 'victim,' " Sue added over the noise of the milk steamer.

Alex ignored them both and kept on going, "I'm not saying that you did. I'm saying that I can vouch that you left before I did. Megan probably can vouch for when you got home, and as the time it takes for you to drive home can also be proven, you should have a clear alibi if worst comes to worst. So Tim, don't worry about it."

Sue handed Tim his drink and he sipped some of the froth while he pondered what Alex had said. "I suppose you're right, but I'm still going to contact my lawyer."

Susan was fishing out Tim's change from the open register as she asked, "So Tim has an alibi, but Alex, do you?"

Alex thought for a second then admitted, "Not a very tight one. I don't have money for a lawyer either, but I have nothing to hide."

"Just don't talk to him then," Tim advised. "You don't even have to be in the same space unless they arrest you, remember that."

Alex knew that to be true, but found that a meeting between her and the detective had to happen at some time in the near future. It was inevitable. She just didn't realize how soon that actual meeting would be.

Chapter 11

Back to work behind the deli counter once again, Alex was busy slicing meats for a customer. She had already sliced the turkey and salami he had asked for and was just starting on the ham. She had had to open a new one to fill the order which she didn't mind too much—at least it wasn't roast beef. That stuff, when freshly opened, was so bloody it looked like the cow had been alive only moments before! Opening new hams and turkeys wasn't so bad, although every time she took her knife to cut the hams in half to create a flat side suitable to slice on she was reminded of what it must be like to cut through a limb, missing the bone of course. As she was sawing away at the chunk of meat, Mr. Bartley suddenly appeared at the counter.

"Hello, Alex," he greeted. "Detective Steiner has a few questions for you, if you wouldn't mind stepping into the office with me?"

Alex stammered an assent, suddenly nervous to be called upon so abruptly, turned over her slicing project to someone else, and followed Nate into his office where three chairs and the detective were waiting. Nate took the chair next to the agent, but before she could take hers Aubrey was out of his own and extending a welcoming hand in her direction, "Detective Steiner, ma'am. I hope you won't mind answering some questions. It seems that you were one of the last people to see Sean alive, and your testimony, although not official, could shed some serious light on the situation. Mr. Bartley, here will be in the room with us, so if you feel uncomfortable—"

Aubrey frowned as Mr. Bartley's private cell phone began to ring shrilly. Nate checked the number and instantly his face started turning crimson, "I'm sorry, but I really have to take this call. I'll be back shortly," and with that he quickly made his way out of the room.

"Or maybe he won't be," Aubrey finished as the door clicked shut. There was a slight note of irritation in his voice, and Alex noticed a slight tremor in his left hand as it lifted to rifle the hair on his head. Aubrey then gestured Alex to her seat while he resumed his own. "If you would like to wait—"

"Actually, Detective Steiner, I have a lot going on back there in the deli; lots of catering orders for the weekend. I'd prefer if we could cut to the chase."

Aubrey nodded and turned to a blank page in his notebook before proceeding with his line of questioning. "Miss Alexandria Hand, how long have you worked here?"

"About two years. And you can call me Alex—everyone else does."

"Did you know if Sean had any enemies? Someone who works, shops, or is a vendor here who might have wanted to hurt him in any way?"

Alex took a genuine moment to think over all the faces she saw come and go over the last few months. Nothing too major stuck out however, and she answered with a simple shake of her head. She went on to ask, "So this was a murder then?"

Aubrey's pen paused. He looked at her for a moment, his face void of any discernible expression, then said calmly, "This is just a routine investigation, ma'am. All un-witnessed deaths need to be explored thoroughly in case of foul play before they can be considered closed."

"And has there been any inclination of foul play?"

"I'm sorry, but I'm not able to reveal the details of the case."

"Oh, sorry," Alex said shyly. She felt her cheeks start to flush and her palms start to sweat. *So this is what an interrogation is like. . . This is so awkward.*

Aubrey cleared his throat and leaned back in his chair, "Sorry for my frankness, but did you ever flirt with Sean, or did Sean ever sexually harass you in any way?"

"What?!" Alex wasn't expecting such a left-fielded question. "Uh, no he didn't—I didn't. Why would you ask that?"

Aubrey shrugged, "I'm trying to follow all different angles. And apparently Sean had a thing for younger ladies. I was just curious if you were one of his slices of pie."

Alex didn't know what to say to that. *Slices of pie? Who the hell is sexually harassing who now?* Suddenly Alex's embarrassment and confusion cleared and were replaced by a tidal wave of anger that landed her back on solid ground. Folding her arms across her chest in a defensive pose she said coldly, "For someone as smart as your bio says you are, you really are an idiot. I know where this is going because I figure I must be a suspect for a couple of reasons. For starters, I was one of the last people to see Sean before he 'moved on,' and secondly I'm sure you ran a background check on all of the people who worked with him, right? Well, as the saying goes you'll catch more flies with honey and unless you change your tactics, this fly isn't going to speak anymore."

Aubrey gave a little bow and gestured to the closed door, "Alright, you don't have to talk. At least not now."

Alex stood to leave but she turned back suddenly, "You know, you should treat the people here with more courtesy. These are all good people who work hard and if Sean was murdered, they would want justice done to the culprit as much as you do." Alex's eyes widened as she witnessed the detective slip a subtle glance at the wall clock. The coffee, the shaky hands, cutting out of work in the early afternoon—she had seen these symptoms too many times before.

Alex's mouth set itself into a grim line as she added meanly, "Although it seems you're more concerned with getting home to start your happy hour rather than solving a possibly heinous crime such as this one! You should be ashamed of yourself!"

Aubrey's eyes flashed as he leapt from his chair, "Listen little lady, nobody is innocent, especially these people you're working with. Like the quote states: 'Virtue is always a lack of opportunity or the product of fear—never a real inclination.' Personally I *do* think Sean was murdered, you want to know why? Because from what everyone has told me this guy was a complete bastard and it's always the bastards that naturally live to be one hundred, unless otherwise, purposely disposed. To bad I can't use that little nugget of wisdom as evidence." Alex flinched as the detective thrust one of his business cards into her hands. "Call me if you think of anything else you might want to ridicule me for—or maybe a detail that slipped that pretty little head of yours."

Alex watched as the detective moved passed her and threw open the door before stalking away. She hadn't felt such raw anger in a while, and the force of it left her with a knot in her throat.

Eventually Alex was calm enough to focus back on her work, but she was fuming for quite awhile after her little "interview" was over. She wondered if Detective Steiner would come back with a warrant and if she really was at the top of his suspect list. But that would be idiotic. Besides the fact that she knew she was innocent, there was no way she would be capable of moving Sean's dead weight all over the place! But then again, if all of this was so silly, why had the detective purposely sought her out to taunt? For kicks? To make it look like he was actually working instead of wasting time like he was currently doing?

Alex was out on the sales floor stocking cheese, a cart piled high with various brands resting nearby. Forcing red waxy wheels of Gouda into a neat row, Alex tried to shake her head to clear away her anger, but it stayed where it was. A sudden shove to the receiving doors caught her attention and she looked up to see Spencer walking through, the limp form of the Freddy the Ferret costume draped over his shoulders.

"What are you doing with Freddy?" Alex asked.

Spencer paused and for a moment debated how to answer. Finally he put a finger to his lips and said, "Shhh, you didn't see anything," then continued on his way. When he disappeared behind the metal frame of the canned good aisle, Alex thought she heard someone else exclaim, "Great! I'll go get the ketchup!" but she wasn't too sure.

Rolling her eyes she tried to focus her energy on the project at hand and moved on to stacking wedges of Gruyère next.

Chapter 12

Aubrey didn't sleep well that night. His normal routine of getting blitzed before bed hadn't worked. The accusation of the deli girl had haunted him all the way home and tainted his new tradition. He wasn't what she had implied—he wasn't an alcoholic! The case took top priority like it always did, and so what if he drank a few beers after work? There was nothing wrong with that!

But this time the buzz hadn't been warm and cozy like it normally was and instead of quieting the monsters that liked to pick apart his nerves as they traversed the landscape of his brain, it had somehow given them strength so that his dreams became clear visions of bullet riddled corpses, their wounds draining away blood like a spring time downpour washes away any discernible trace of a muddy river bank. And amongst all of the white and red bodies stood the ghost of Sean, the deli pimp, dressed in green faux fur with a hole in the back of his head and a collection of girls dressed as assorted rotting lunchmeats at his feet asking, "Who killed me kid? Figured it out yet? It's a hot night at the deli—we're running some killer deals! Guess who done it and get the choice cut of meat you want at *half price*! A limited time only! Come one, come all—"

Aubrey jerked awake and barely made it to the bathroom before puking up the contents of his stomach. When there was nothing solid left, thin streams of bile came up, the acidity burning his throat and making his eyes water. After the ordeal was over he sat heavily on the linoleum floor, his breathing ragged and his hands pulling on fistfuls of hair as if with the pain he could also pull the monsters away from their roosts.

~*~*~*~*~

Alex didn't sleep well either which was an annoyance she couldn't afford since she had to open the deli department the next day. Sadly, her alarm clock would be ringing at 4:30 a.m., a measly five hours away. . .

Nevertheless, she was so pissed about the way that know-it-all detective had treated not only her, but the other co-workers he had questioned! Apparently Alex and Tim weren't the only ones he was rude to. But after asking around, Alex found that his bad attitude had been selective, as if to purposely get a rise out of certain targets for some reason that she couldn't identify other than maybe for the detective's own amusement.

And that quote! There had been a minor spark of recognition as he had spoken it, and as the day wore on she was positive she had heard it somewhere. When she asked the others who worked around her they had denied ever hearing such a saying before, but by the time she got out of work the coffee shop was closed, along with the library, and she hadn't felt it so important that she needed to stop at a 24-hour McDonald's or a friends house to verify it. At least not at first.

As the night continued and sleep eluded her, Alex finally focused on that dumb quote and came awake suddenly with the knowledge that it came from a book—a now very rare book by one of her favorite authors—a Mr. Frank Yerby. She had discovered the African-American author when she had looked through the multitude of books she had inherited after her parents' demise and had fallen in love with his flowing sentences and charming characters and places of America in the 1800's. He had written thirty-three books that went to print as well as a bunch of others that didn't. Considered to be the "King of the Costume Novel" Mr. Yerby was the first African-American to have a best-selling novel as well as a Hollywood film contract. . . But that had been three years ago when she had plowed through the hard covered backings; a long time to remember a specific quote from a specific book.

However, she did remember the basic plot of the text and had a shadowy sense of the characters. Paging through the nine volumes of her Yerby collection she finally came upon the specific passage about virtue from the novel, *A Woman Called Fancy*.

Alex smiled as she reread the words that she herself had underlined at their first reading. At the time she had felt that these words were a true nugget of wisdom, and had been amused by the negative light they lit up the world with. But now when her own world was threatened by such negativity and at the fact that the man who this time had spoken them must also believe them to be true, Alex felt a bit sad. Was the world really that evil? Were innocence and virtue simply lies to the real world?

Alex tried to shake away these thoughts. Smiling to herself she said, "I can't believe he's read one of Yerby's works. Maybe he isn't such an idiot after all."

Alex walked slowly back to her room and took a seat on her bed, setting the novel gently down on her nightstand next to the detective's card. She took the card into her hand and flipped it over. It was a boring thing really, one-sided with the detective's full name, office location, and other contact information.

Call me if you think of anything else you might want to ridicule me for—or maybe a detail that slipped that pretty little head of yours, he had said. Not exactly the normal cliché, cop-like phrase one gets, but then he wasn't like any of the other cops Alex had ever met. He obviously had some kind of chip on his shoulder—and he wasn't trying too hard to hide it from the world either.

Suddenly another random thought slammed to the forefront of her mind.

"The bell!" she cried aloud. "That back door bell! It sounded just as I was leaving! That means I wasn't the last person to talk to Sean after all!"

Alex was grabbing for her cell phone when she saw that her analogue clock read 1:15 and despairingly, she hesitated. "I guess it'll have to wait until tomorrow."

Chapter 13

Alex didn't mind opening. And overall she was used to doing it with only a few hours of sleep. Going from night shifts most of the week to a sudden morning shift was taxing to one's soul, but Alex bore it as best as she could—normally with the aid of an insane amount of caffeine.

She arrived that Saturday morning at 5:30 and clocked in fifteen minutes later. While making her way back to her department, Alex found no signs of any "bread ghost"—not that she really believed in any such nonsense, but it was a calming balm to see that everything was as she had left it the night before; no flickering lights, random dirty dishes sitting in the sinks, or loaves of bread sitting idly beneath their designated shelves. Other than herself, a bakery, and a front desk associate, no one was around and everything was quiet when the doors officially opened at 6 a.m..

By 7:00 things started to pick up. Early risers came to buy baked goods to eat with their already purchased coffee from next door, a few department managers trickled in, and reinforcements for deli, grocery, and the meat counter sluggishly entered to start the day's production quota.

However, today wasn't going to be a normal Saturday. Today there was an event planned to happen throughout the store—a Chocolate and Wine Tasting event with multiple tables set up inviting customers to partake in Forestgrove Grocery's finest delights. This event had been scheduled for some time, but without Sean to supervise the festivities, Claire (who had worked the department the longest) had been shoved into his place to help vendors set up and get situated. That's why Alex had to open—to make sure the deli department was properly attended.

By 8:00 the store was a madhouse. There were managers from various departments scrambling to find enough tables to set up. It seemed no one could find the disposable wine glasses, and there was a fight about to break out between a local cheese vendor and a local honey producer over their designated spots. It seemed they were both told to set up in the same location.

Alex stood calmly behind her deli counter, taking it all in while making sandwiches to fill up the grab-and-go case, waiting patiently for the true chaos to begin like she knew it would (this wasn't her first rodeo) with Blaire, normally a weekday, morning person, prepping the salad bar near by.

"I love days like today," Alex said. "The bustle gives the air a touch of electricity, the people tend to be nicer because they're actually here to have a good time (maybe also because they've been drinking) and because there's all this free food and alcohol! There aren't many other jobs where you can get away with drinking at work! Moderate drinking, of course"

"I guess, yeah," Blaire replied boringly. "I just hope we don't get too busy."

Getting 'too busy' turned out to be an understatement. Normally on a weekend there were only two people scheduled in the morning and two more scheduled at night in the deli, with all four people working over the lunch hour. Well, even with Claire sometimes stopping by to help out between directing customers and vendors, they could have used three more people.

There was no chef on the weekends either, so Alex became the designated cook over the lunch hours during which she was given twenty different orders (an average of three sandwiches per ticket) within ten minutes from violently hungry guests, and plowed them out order by order in an almost superhuman twenty-five minutes.

She also played busser, meat slicer, salad bar cleaner, and GPS for lost guests looking for the bathrooms that were clearly labeled as being in the front of the store. At one point while bringing out an order for a BLT and a Rueben, Alex had to swerve through a maze of bakery speed-racks holding cooling pans of cookies and breads, dip under an extended phone line, and dodge an assortment of bodies, before finally reaching the table where the expecting customers sat. On her way back to the deli she couldn't help but laugh to herself, "God, I feel like Indiana Jones some days!" Even as a lowly deli worker, there were times when you could get an adrenaline rush of sorts.

Most of the customers were single identities picking up bouquets of roses, boxes of chocolate, cards, and supplies for romantic dinners like the chocolate-rubbed herb crusted tenderloins currently on sale, along with sides of freshly grilled asparagus, sautéed scallops and steamed shrimp. There were also many couples strewn about, feeding each other chocolate covered strawberry halves, and taking sips from each other's samples of wine. The couples were all dressed smartly, most of the women wearing large engagement or wedding rings. Alex felt a tiny stab of regret of not having anyone to enjoy this crazy holiday with, but quickly pushed the feeling aside. She was aware of the history behind V-day, and was currently too busy to think of such frivolous things.

Valentine's Day was a holiday first celebrated in Rome, honoring the god Lupercus, the protector from wolves. Every year the Roman's would throw a feast to celebrate the god as well as the coming spring and fertility.

During this feast, couples would be randomly paired together. Sometimes the matches led to marriage.

But, in an attempt to banish away all pagan holidays, the Christian religion used the martyrdom of St. Valentine to create a new holiday. However, it didn't work exactly as planned. The Roman's loved to celebrate *Lupercalia* and they continued to do so until eventually Valentine's Day became so jumbled that it became known as a holiday of love, big pink hearts, and half-naked babies carrying crossbows. Alex thought V-day was one of the dumbest holidays ever. She normally made it a point to dress in black on the 14th, and wasn't going to let any sort of longing for romantic gestures change her way of thinking.

It turned out that for some reason (the weather maybe?) that the people who had come in for the samplings weren't all friendly. In fact, some of them were quite over demanding. One person practically screamed for someone to help them just because no one behind the counter walked over during their first second of arrival. Another complained that all the salads looked 'old,' and couldn't bear the thought of tasting any. And still another scoffed at the idea that freshly made, hot sandwiches should take any more than five minutes to make. . . That special someone then claimed to have waited fifteen minutes for her lunch, when in fact it had only been seven and a half, and refused to pay for anything. Alex let Claire handle that one.

At one point an elderly gentleman came up to the counter bringing with him a random assortment of goat cheeses. When Alex walked over he said, "I can't find the address on these things. The print is too small!"

Alex picked up one of the packages and glanced at it, "Are you looking for an address to go visit there or something?"

The man shouted, "Yes! I want to see the goats! They have 800 goats at the farm, along with a factory and a cheese store, and I want to see them! I want to see the goats!"

Alex tried very hard to keep her professional demeanor, "But this *is* the company you're looking to visit? MontChevrè, correct?"

"No!" Shouted the man. "I know it's none of these cheeses, but the farm with all of the goats is here in Wisconsin. If I hear the name then I'll know it. It's somewhere north of here."

Alex blinked at the man. *If you don't recall the name of the company then how can I help you find an address for it? And why did you have to bring me all of these wedges of cheese?* Suddenly another popular brand of goat cheese that the store sold popped into her head. "Sir, are you looking for the LaClare Farms?"

"Yes! They're the ones with the 800 goats!"

"Alright Sir, that stuff is located in a cheese bunker over this way. Let's go see if there's an address for you. . ."

Not all of the customers were annoying. In fact, a lot of Alex's regulars came in just to do their weekly shopping and made it a point to stop by. There was the lady who just couldn't pass up the Peanut Butter Stack Snacks; Kim (whose name she discovered is Welsh for "chief"), the tennis instructor, who came every Saturday for his salad bar rations and ice water; the family with the four kids—all with glasses on their small, cute faces; and the guy originally from Serbia whom Alex could spend hours with talking about books. It was these people that really kept her working at the grocery store instead of looking for a job with more money or better benefits. They made the place feel like one big family, and made the weird, snotty, and rude customers seem not so bad.

But today even Alex's regulars weren't enough to color the day in a positive light.

The morning, which had started so serenely and slowly turned sour, was completed by the stupidity of a gentleman looking to buy a cake for his wife for Valentine's Day. He approached Alex with a perplexed look on his face and asked, "Could you tell me what kind of cake this is? It doesn't say."

Alex glanced at the cake in his hands. It was frosted and shaped to look like one of those dogs you might put inside a purse, with fluffy white frosting as fur, and a plastic bow sitting between its drooping ears. It was one of the cutest things Alex had seen in awhile.

"It doesn't say on the tag on the bottom, does it?"

The guy took a moment to glance under the box and then again looked at Alex, shaking his head.

Alex internally sighed and took the box gently away from him, lifting it high so she could get a better look at the thing. Clearly printed on the label was: *Chocolate Dog Cake $7.99.*

Alex felt an intense anger at this gentleman's folly and she had to work really hard to keep it at bay as she said sweetly, "This is a chocolate cake sir. A really cute one. I hope you'll enjoy it."

The guy took the cake and went on his way. Alex turned to the clock and noticed the beginnings of a headache coming on. It was finally 2:30 in the afternoon. Finally she could go home—but first she needed to find that detective and tell him about the back door thing. She had noticed him just a couple of times moving about the store, making it a point to stop at every liquor and wine station as he went.

Alex figured he would still be lurking around somewhere—especially if there were free drinks about. Either way, the alcoholism part really wasn't her concern. Informing him about the late night visitor was.

As she gathered her things and wished the others "good luck," she was hoping he wouldn't keep her too long and praying that he wouldn't be an ass this time.

Chapter 14

Aubrey was awakened about seven-thirty in the morning on the 12th by an unexpected phone call. Nate, enraged and spooked about something or other, yelled into his ear for five minutes before Aubrey was able to sneak in a "I'll be over there soon!" and was able to hang up. Apparently the murderer in question had struck again.

Scrambling to get dressed and speeding with his police lights flashing atop his dashboard, Aubrey was able to reach the grocery store in record time. He had called in to dispatch on the way there, but as he neared the store something in his stomach started to ache. He tried to place where his uneasiness was coming from, when suddenly it dawned on him—there was no one panicking. There were no loose crowds of employees and early risers gathered out front, waiting for the police to arrive. Instead there was a quarter-filled parking lot with a mother and son casually making their way to the entrance in order to purchase groceries. Everything seemed normal—too normal.

Confused, Aubrey parked his truck and turned the lights off. Walking into the store he grabbed the first employee he came across and asked where Mr. Bartley was. "In his office, I think," came the meek reply.

Aubrey was about to put his hand on the door handle when the office door opened and out came Nate, his face red with irritation. "It's about time you got here! Look what they did to my office!"

Nate stood aside so that Aubrey could get a better look and instantly Aubrey's shoulders drooped and his concern turned to irritation, then embarrassment. "Excuse me a minute, Mr. Bartley," Aubrey said while quickly whipping out his phone and dialing the direct line to dispatch. *God,*

*please let me reach them in time to call off the backup! I'll
never hear the end of this otherwise.*

"Hey Trudy, can you cancel that last alert to
Forestgrove Grocery? Yeah, it's an all clear. Tell the guys
I'm sorry, alright? Yeah, I'll explain when I check in later.
Thanks, Trudy. Bye."

Placing the phone back into his pocket Aubrey took
another long glance into the manager's office and asked
Bartley sternly from over his shoulder, "I thought you told
me on the phone that the murderer stuck again? I thought you
were calling in another body, not a prank!"

Nate's face turned a darker shade of red as he tried
desperately to keep his voice at a moderate level, "When I
walked in there this morning I almost had a heart attack,
okay? What was I supposed to think, I mean the sign around
its neck. . .?"

Aubrey sighed and walked further into the room.
Someone had taken a great deal of time working out the
details of this little display. All of the fluorescent lights had
red tissue paper covering them, casting the room in a hellish
tone. In Nate's office chair sat Freddy the Ferret, his eyes,
teeth, and claws smeared with some sort of red substance.
Placing his head closer, Aubrey took a whiff, and then used a
finger to scrape at the substance. It easily peeled off in a
goopy mess. Around Freddy's furry little neck hung a sign
written in red marker that read: IT WAS ME! I DID IT!
CAREFUL OR YOU MIGHT BE NEXT!

Aubrey heaved another sigh and couldn't help but
smile. It would have scared him shitless too, especially
coming into work at such an annoying hour as 5 a.m.. It was
a great prank. But it did make him wonder if it hadn't been
intended to scare *him*, and not the boss man.

Rubbing his eyes, Aubrey walked back to Nate who stood with arms crossed over his chest. "So now what? I know it's not a body, but it's almost the same thing. I mean, someone defiled the store's private property! You need to hurry up and get to the bottom of this investigation before anything else gets damaged! Do you even have any leads yet?"

"Mr. Bartley, I'm doing the best that I can, and honestly, I'm almost out of your hair. I have a few more interviews to do. That's it. As for the people who did this—" Aubrey said, jabbing a thumb toward Freddy, "I would check to see who was working last night and go from there. This has nothing to do with the Sean Ritter case, other than an attempt to delay the investigation, which I do not intend to do."

"What do you mean that it isn't related? What about the blood on Freddy's—"

"Mr. Bartley, that's ketchup. And no "murderer" is going to put tissue paper over the lights just to 'add to the effect.' This was a prank, nothing more."

"Detective Steiner—"

"Mr. Bartley, I'll be back in an hour or two. I left my notes and things at home in my hurry to get here. We can talk more about his later, alright?"

"Hey Steiner, everything okay here?"

Aubrey closed his eyes and suppressed a groan. The speaker was behind him but from the heavy sounding treads, clinks of keys and other items from their utility belts, and the familiar drawl, Aubrey had a vague idea of who it was.

Plastering a smile on his face, Aubrey turned, "Hey

Bill, Charlie. Yes, everything is just fine. Didn't you guys get the call to desist?"

Both Bill and Charlie were your stereotypical policemen—overweight, laid back, and always looking for a way to harass the rookies. Between chews on the Double Bubble wad in his mouth Charlie explained, "We were pulling into the lot when Trudy radioed the all clear, false alarm, but we figured since we were already here that we'd check to see if there was anything we could help you with."

"Well that's mighty nice of you," Aubrey said, trying his best to not say the words in a mock country-hick accent. "But like I said—everything is just fine."

"Everything is *not* fine!" Mr. Bartley snapped. My office has been vandalized and my person threatened and Detective Steiner here plans to do nothing about it!"

A look passed between the newcomers before their glances turned questioningly to Aubrey.

Aubrey let out a large sigh and ran a hand through his hair. "Mr. Bartley," he said weakly, "You've been victim of a prank, nothing more. There's no need to—"

"Pranked?" Bill asked, a smile pulling at the corners of his lips.

"Maybe if we take a look to, uh, help properly assess the situation, would that put you at ease, Mr. Bartley?" Charlie asked.

Nate nodded, "I would appreciate that."

Charlie turned to Aubrey, "That alright with you? Bill and I wouldn't want to step on any toes."

Biting the inside of his cheek Aubrey shook his head

and gestured toward the office door, "Go ahead, 'properly assess' all you want."

With a mask of seriousness covering all but the amusement in their eyes, both Bill and Charlie entered the room and took their time examining the scene. Finally, Charlie (the more diplomatic of the two) came out, put an arm around Mr. Bartley, and, talking softly, led him slightly away. Aubrey could see Bill's huge bulk shaking from laughter in the door frame. As he passed Aubrey he winked and said under his breath, "Looks like you have a vermin problem. Gunna need a good exterminator for that one."

Aubrey stifled an unprofessional urge and gave a dry chuckle instead. *God, I'm never going to hear the end of this, am I?*

~*~*~*~*~

Even though he wouldn't be able to keep the Freddy disaster from the others at the Cop Shop, Bill and Charlie were helpful in calming Mr. Bartley down enough to finally accept that it had probably been a harmless joke after all, and eventually Aubrey was able to run home quick and gather his notes.

When he made it back to the store, Aubrey was surprised by all of the excitement in the air as he watched managers and vendors hurrying this way and that, trying to set up some sort of event with free samples. The atmosphere had drastically changed since this morning's adventure, and even Nate seemed to be in a more charming mood now that his office was vermin free.

While the vendors were setting up Aubrey meandered through, dropping vague questions about whether they had ever worked directly with Sean or not, and if they did what impressions they had of him. Most of them had been vendors there before Sean had even attained his position, but they didn't know exactly who Aubrey was referring to until they received the added description of "tall, thin, very business-like, a very fast talker and walker." After that bit of information (which Aubrey had plagiarized from one of the breakfasters he had talked to a couple days ago), then came the nods and slight smiles, but there was nothing more to say than, "Oh yeah, he was really professional, but I never really dealt with him in person, only through phone calls or e-mails." Claire Debauch seemed to be everyone's primary contact if they needed anything.

Aubrey's mood greatly improved as he went from table to table, enjoying samples of the various products. There were local cheeses, freshly made jams, a variety of cooked meats, and lots of alcohol to taste. The Great Lakes Distillery made one powerful whiskey. And the Door County wines were refreshingly sweet on the tongue. He didn't care too much for the hard root beer, but imagined it might make an awesome root beer float if you added just a dollop of RumChata.

Without the need to stop for a lunch break, Aubrey asked Nate to accompany him into the private office while he talked to his first Forestgrove Grocery associate of the day: Mrs. Julie Nikles.

Julie was in her late thirties, but wore so much makeup and fashionable clothes—the correct way—that it made her look ten years younger; a modern miracle that would make any woman jealous. Her interview started off smoothly, but before he was able to really delve into more serious questions about the missing money or about Sean's love life, Julie suddenly broke into tears.

Through over-dramatic sobs Julie cried, "Sean wasn't the best guy around. I mean, he could really be a prick, but he was at least competent! And he was my work husband so I got to see that caring side of his too, unlike most of the others."

"Work husband? What is that?" Aubrey asked. Even Nate seemed disturbed about this sudden outbreak.

"I mean, we weren't doing anything against company policy," she said while looking directly at Nate. Turning to Aubrey she added, "We just leaned on each other when things got too stressful around here. A while ago he helped me quite smoking. I bet he would be pretty disappointed to learn that I started up again. . ."

"Well, being his 'work wife,' did you ever see any recent projects he was working on or did you notice him hanging out with certain people while he was here at the store?"

Julie shook her head, but then burst out with a fresh batch of tears, "He was always planning something! I always wondered when that man actually went to bed because he would stay here so late, and sometimes come in extra early to get things done. A couple weeks before he died he told me he discovered an error of some sort in the financial records, but didn't explain further. He was really excited and said he was planning something big. When I tried to ask what the big plan was, he said he couldn't tell me yet, but if it all worked out the way he wanted it to, that everything would change around here."

When Julie was dismissed Aubrey sat back in his chair and eyed Nate suspiciously, "Well that was interesting, 'An error of some sort in the financial records?' Any way you would let me have a free look at those or be able to elaborate further?"

Mr. Bartley cleared his throat, but Aubrey couldn't

tell if it meant anything, "Of course you can. I'll let you have my password to the financial files (we store them all on the computer now), but honestly, Detective Steiner, if you want my opinion, Julie is—" Nate paused, tossing his head while he tried to conjure up the right word. "—She's a little dumb. She's great with people, but without young Timothy out there, Julie could barely run a register let alone know the difference between the reports we keep. Now, what I think Sean stumbled upon was the error he brought to my attention about the inventory sheets from December." Nate paused and moved to his computer where he shook the mouse to awaken it. Typing in his password he said, "Now if we just pull those up, maybe I can help you see what Sean saw and was determined to change."

A few seconds later Nate had pulled up the inventory sheets and pointed to a few areas highlighted in red. "See what I mean?" he asked.

Aubrey nodded, "This actually lights a different, totally unrelated light bulb in my head, but for now I'd like to keep it on the back burner. I also don't want to spook anyone just yet." Aubrey looked down at the list of people he wanted to talk to today and selected another uncrossed name from it. "Let's talk to Miss Cyndi Miller from the bakery department next. Then maybe we'll make a move on that guy."

Chapter 15

"Hey, is that detective guy still here?" Alex asked as she reached the courtesy desk.

Tim was working today too. He had a long line of people but took the time to answer tartly, "Yes. He's in the office with Nate and Evan from meat department doing another 'interview.' "

Alex thanked him and went into the break room to clock out. She was planning on waiting just outside the office door so that she could catch the detective as soon as he was finished, but the sound of someone crying made her hang back.

Walking further into the break room she found Cyndi weeping and sniffling somewhat heavily. "Hey, what happened?" Alex asked, alarmed.

It took a few minutes for Cyndi to calm down enough for her to be understandable. Her crying eventually dwindled. "I talked to that guy," she said through hiccups, "—that detective guy." Cyndi shook her head, "And I told him about Evan and me—right in front of Nate, and now I think they're firing him! Either that or I'll have to quit. This is just like what happened to Parker and Kristy! Oh, Alex, I need this job! I have a kid to support because his father's such a loser—you know that!"

"Cyndi, calm down. I doubt they would fire him just because you two are dating."

"But it's against company policy that a manager and a minion—"

Alex put a hand on Cyndi's arm, "They're probably just giving him a slap on the wrist or something." There was a pause and then she asked curiously, "How did they get you to tell them about you two? I thought you were hardcore about keeping it all a secret."

Cyndi nodded and began to explain what happened, "We were yes, but I was going to be pegged with murder! I was working that night and according to the detective, that unless I could come up with an alibi, I was a main suspect. He was going to take me in if I didn't tell them about Evan!"

"Did he really say that? That's not true. He couldn't take you in with such a lame excuse!"

They both froze as the door to the break room was slammed against the wall and a furious Evan, his hands cuffed behind him, came bursting through. "You bitch!" he screamed at Cyndi. "You ratted me out!"

Two local policemen hurried after him, grabbing him before he could take more than three steps from the doorway and started to drag the struggling Evan backwards.

"No, baby, I would never—"

"Ratted you out for what?" Alex asked, confused, as she watched the drama unfold.

The two officers were able to move Evan out of the doorway and out toward the exit where no doubt a transport was waiting. Aubrey and another man entered. Flashing his ID which tagged him as another detective from the Sheboygan Police Force, the new face stepped up to Cyndi and said kindly, "Ma'am, I'm Detective Joey Hanks, and if you wouldn't mind coming with me, we have a few questions we'd like to ask you down at the station about your 'friend,' Evan Sanderson."

Alex could see Cyndi's whole body shake as she

stood and went with the officer.

"Remember, you don't have to say anything!" she heard herself shout after her friend's trembling form.

"You aren't going to law school or something, are you?" Alex was so preoccupied that she hadn't realized Detective Steiner was standing right next to her, or even that she herself was standing. "Don't worry; she's not under suspicion for anything major. More than likely she didn't even know about the under the table dealings that have been going on."

"What 'under the table dealings?' " Alex asked.

"Between the inventory records taken for December and January, and a tattoo matching the description of eye-witness reports, it seems that your meat manager was stealing lobster tails and selling them at bars."

"What?" Alex asked in disbelief. "That's a thing?"

"Apparently," was his reply before taking his leave of the break room. Alex didn't follow right away. She was still dumbfounded by this new revelation. "Wait, does that mean he's the murderer too?"

Aubrey turned to her and shrugged, "My gut tells me that Mr. Sanderson doesn't have what it takes to kill someone, but you never know—and the Ritter case still cannot be confirmed as a murder. Of course we'll learn more as Hanks and his team question him."

Both of them were out of the break room when Mr. Bartley came barreling down upon them, "This is just great. Couldn't you have handled that with more stealth? Busiest day so far this year and you have to go and take away two more of my employees!"

Aubrey's manner was defensive as he said, "Hey, I just discovered who it was that was stealing your seafood! You should be thanking me right now."

"But you had him arrested during my event! Did you know that *The Kohlers* were here when your little friends whisked my meat manager away?! Mr. Steiner, my store caters to the rich and high status of the area and I can't have this kind of outrage happening! At least not right in front of their noses!"

Alex thought she had never heard Nate's voice so loud and angry before. If Aubrey had made a scene, Nate was giving a show.

"And what are you doing, Mr. Bartley?" Aubrey asked quietly, his cheeks red and eyes narrow. "Are you practicing for your comedy hour? A man might have been murdered—"

"And we're all very sorry that he is gone, but I've watched as you bullied and harassed my employees, ruffled my customers, made a mockery of me, and I'll have no more of it! I'm going to call your superiors—"

Aubrey shook his head and smiled sarcastically at the man before him and said fiercely, "I was just doing my job. It's not my fault you suck at yours." He then turned and left the store.

This time Alex thought it best to let him go.

Chapter 16

Aubrey made a beeline to his truck and started the engine even before his door slammed closed. "Who the fuck does that guy think he is, huh? Lobster-man stole seven hundred fucking dollars worth of supplies so far and I can't even get a simple 'thank you?' Jeezus fuuucking Christ!" He slammed an open palm on the steering wheel and revved out of the parking lot.

Aubrey's whole body felt like it was on fire. He either needed to punch something, or get a drink down fast. The closest rat hole of a bar was five minutes away, but he made it there in two. Walking rigidly in he noticed it was called *The Bitter End* and laughed darkly to himself, "What a fitting name." There were only three or four others present besides the bartender, who was an older, fat man with a grease stain on the front of his shirt. Aubrey took a stool at the bar, one with his back to a wall and where he could see the door—a habit he had developed during cop school—and immediately ordered a shot of Single Barrel Jack.

As he waited he caught a glimpse of the clock above the bar which declared in a brilliant red glow that it was only 2:53 in the afternoon. He shifted uncomfortably in his seat. *I'm not an alcoholic. There's nothing wrong with downing a couple—besides it's saving someone from getting their face caved in—a complete dunce that can't even tell the difference between real blood and frickin' ketchup!*

The shot was quick enough to arrive but Aubrey didn't drink it right away. Instead he took the small glass into his hands and gazed into the dark liquid, totally engrossed in his own thoughts.

I should never have become a cop. I can convince people to show me their skeletons, but only by making them itch—by confusing them so that they can't figure out which way is up. By making me *the bad guy. . . Since when did cops have to become the bad guys? Or were they always that way?* Aubrey sighed deeply and continued his reverie. *I never wanted to be a policeman; that was dad's big dream—to have the lineage of law enforcers continue through the Steiner clan. "We're big important men, us Steiners! Make the family proud, son!"*

Then what did you want to be?

I don't know. . .

> *You didn't have a clue what to do with your life. You went along with your father's pushing, and you know it. You can't blame this on him! Your classes made clear that the policeman's job isn't a pocket of rainbows. They all warned you how difficult it can be!*

They never told me how mentally jarring it is. . . How alone you might feel. How much guilt could be laid on your shoulders at anytime—or how often you have to put aside your own feelings, just to put on that mask of empathy for, or even acceptance of all of the filth of the world. . .

Besides, there's no glory in this damn job! You might make a drug bust or put a killer away, but there's always more. And its not only never-ending, but everyone hates you for putting away their child, their lover. They hate you for taking away their lousy, thieving employees and making them look bad in front of their betters!

Aubrey started when the phone in his pocket began to vibrate. Nate had gotten around to calling his supervisor sooner than expected. Best scenario, Helmer would be calling to find out what had happened. Worse one would be that Aubrey was pulled from the case. *Best to get this over with,* he thought to himself as he answered the ring and put the phone up to his ear.

"Look Captain, I know you're upset, but at least listen to my side before you decide—"

The person on the other line butted in awkwardly, "Um, I'm sorry, but is this Detective Steiner's phone? It's Alexandria Hand, from Forestgrove Grocery. . . I was hoping we could meet because I remembered something that might help find my ex-boss's possible killer?"

Aubrey was bewildered at the fact that it was not his boss on the other end, and mentally kicked himself for not answering his phone more professionally. He was about to respond when a patron must have ordered the special drink of the house or something and the bartender reached over and rang the huge metal bell that was suspended only a yard away from Aubrey's head. The resounding CLANG was so loud and unexpected that Aubrey visibly flinched and gave a startled cry into the phone.

While trying to recover, Aubrey heard laughter from the girl on the other end as she exclaimed, "Oh, you're at *The Bitter End*, aren't you? I've had that same reaction a couple of times myself. I'll be right there!"

Aubrey was going to protest and suggest they meet somewhere more appropriate but she had already hung up. "Guess I'll just have to wait here." He then motioned the bartender back over and flashed him his badge. With a clear warning audible in his voice he said, "Don't do that ever again while I'm here, understand?"

The bartender nodded and retreated to his more friendly patrons sitting on the opposite side of the bar.

Chapter 17

Alex arrived shortly after she had hung up. His reaction to the bell ringing had been humorous enough for her to ignore her disgust at the fact that the detective had gone directly to a bar after his earlier confrontation. *What he does when he isn't working really isn't any of my business,* she kept thinking to herself. *Besides I still need to tell him about that late night visitor at the back door.*

She hadn't had time to go home and change so before entering the bar she discarded her hat and apron. The rest of her uniform was mostly covered by her winter jacket, but there really wasn't much she could do about her hat hair without a brush. She shrugged and opened her car door. *It's not like I'm going on a date or anything.*

Inside, the atmosphere was dim except for the light from a few gambling machines and two big screen TV's that were focused on recapturing the highlights of the sports world. The swirling spirals of smoke from cigarettes would have been apparent if the Wisconsin law prohibiting smoking in public spaces hadn't been passed a few years ago; however, the smell still lingered faintly.

Alex spotted the detective on the far side of the bar, and took note of the shot glass clutched in his left hand. He gave a slight wave with his right and she made her way over swiftly. Maybe because she was the only woman present so far, but the bartender appeared as if by magic and kindly asked if she needed anything. She responded nicely in return for a Wisconsin original: Whiskey Old Fashioned, sour, and with cherries instead of olives. She then settled herself onto the stool next to the detective and entered into an awkward zone of silence.

But Aubrey quickly breached that zone by asking,

"So you're a whiskey girl, huh?"

Alex smiled, "Yup, and I can hold it well too. Both of my grandpa's were alcoholics. I inherited those important qualities from them."

"Spoken like a true Wisconsinite," Aubrey paused before asking not unkindly, "So is that why you branded me as one of those yesterday? An alcoholic?"

Alex received her drink and sipped it slowly before answering, "No. I've experienced someone else who possessed the symptoms of one, which since you've read my file, I'm sure you are already aware of that specific life event."

"You mean your ex-boyfriend who you assaulted in self-defense because he was trying to beat you to death with a baseball bat? Yes, I did read that report."

Alex bristled slightly at his candor and frowned. "He was actually my ex-fiancée." She sighed at the thought of having to repeat her grisly tale, but decided that it was best out in the open. "It was Halloween night and we had just gotten home from a party. We had both been drinking, although I drank far less than he. He had just finished proposing and I had said yes. . . but with the condition that he stop drinking. We started fighting, he starting hitting me, he picked up the first thing he could get his hands on and I knew right then and there that he was going to kill me. So I did what I had to do to protect myself." Alex had retold her story without much infliction, just a flat voice which held hardly any emotion and with eyes focused solely on her glass. When she had finished she looked Aubrey straight in the eye and added, "So forgive me if I don't appreciate those who abuse their liquor."

"I'm sorry," Aubrey answered with a sincere apology

in his voice. "I promise you I'm not normally so rude and I don't normally come to places like this and drink myself into a stupor—at least not this early in the day."

Alex gave a small smile, "You must have your excuses. They really aren't my business anyways, so don't worry about it, Detective Steiner. I'll keep my opinions to myself—speaking of which, I'm sorry how Nate treated you today. I don't like how you've been treating me or my friends during your little 'interviews,' but he didn't need to be such a jerk to you."

"Thanks. If you like, you can just call me Aubrey. 'Detective Steiner' is sometimes a mouthful."

There was a moment where no one spoke. Then with a slight smile Alex asked, "So when did you get around to reading Frank Yerby?"

"Huh?"

"Yesterday you told me one of your favorite quotes, remember? About virtue, or the lack thereof. Well I went home last night and was driven basically insane trying to figure out where I had heard that quote before! Then finally I remembered where I had seen it. I dragged out almost a whole bookshelf before finding the correct book it came out of. I'm a huge fan of Yerby's work, although most of it is hard to come by. So where were you exposed to his books?"

Aubrey's mouth had a slight lift to it as he said, "Ah yes, Mr. Frank Yerby. I was grounded a lot as a child, and well, my mom always had a lot of books lying around. So one day I picked one up. I think I read that one in a day, I got hooked so badly."

"I loved how all of his books had the same basic plot of a love triangle."

"But there was always so much more to them! A man who came from nothing but raised himself in society. And there were a lot of historically accurate facts too. That's what kept my attention."

Alex nodded and for a third time they sat together in silence, this time a bit more relaxed as they remembered their personal reading experiences. Alex was about to fill in the space by continuing the topic of favorite authors when Aubrey jumped in hesitantly, "So on the phone you said you had something you needed to tell me?"

Alex shook her head, angry at herself. She couldn't believe she had almost forgotten for a second time why she had come here to talk to him. She set her drink down on the counter and swiveled so her whole body faced him, "Yes. I forgot about it before, and sadly, again now—it was such a small thing—but on the night of the murder—"

"We still can't rule this one as a murder—"

"—Yeah, yeah, anyways, that night as I was leaving I heard the back door buzzer go off. I was going to go and let that person in—the door is locked from the outside after 4 p.m.—but left it for Sean to answer instead." Alex paused, a new glint in her eyes while Aubrey just sat there, staring at her. "Don't you get it? That means that I wasn't the last person to talk to Sean while he was alive! Someone, the murderer perhaps, came to the back of the store when everyone else should have been gone, and Sean let him in! I figure this mystery person had to have a meeting planned with Sean and then planned to kill him, or person X forgot something and the killing was an accident."

Aubrey sat up straight with this news. "This is a revelation then. Damn those budget cuts! Because of those we don't have any camera shots!"

"Wait, all of those security cameras are turned off? That's just stupid!"

"Tell me about it. All but the ones by the front doors and the expensive alcohol are just for show. Hmmm, this fact does make the murder angle a larger possibility, but it doesn't narrow down my suspect list any further."

Over the rim of her glass Alex said, "Of course it does. Not many people park in the back lot, mostly because they aren't allowed." Alex had Aubrey's rapt attention now. "Only managers and catering people get to park in the back. So more than likely they parked there out of habit, rather than anything else."

"Yes, but that's just speculation." Aubrey and Alex were silent for a spell, before Aubrey said excitedly, "Or maybe person X knew about the cameras and parked in the back purposely! This person must also have known that everyone else would be gone that late at night. So if Sean was murdered, this fact proves that it was someone he definitely knew and didn't consider a threat, and to know about the cameras, person X definitely would have to work at Forestgrove Grocery. At least I can give the Navy buddies and the jealous wife angle a rest for now."

"You keep saying "if" Sean was murdered. Wasn't there any forensic evidence that could steer you either way?"

Aubrey hesitated before answering. He knew he shouldn't be divulging any details about the open investigation—mainly because there were so few of them. Plus, Alex's story could be totally made up just to get her in the clear. His gut instincts didn't consider this girl to be threatening in any way, and having a consultant on the case who knew the inner workings of Forestgrove Grocery would be helpful. . .

"There wasn't much gained by the autopsy," he said, keeping her in neutral territory for now. "Although we did find a pin in the freezer lying next to the body—maybe you could help me identify if the pin belonged to the deceased?"

Aubrey pulled out his phone once again and noticed that he had two missed calls from the station that he hadn't even noticed due to his excitement over this tiny, yet crucial new puzzle piece. He pressed the ignore button for now and went into his photo gallery where he had kept some of the evidence pictures handy for situations such as this.

The picture he pulled up was of a faux gold pin no more than ¾ of an inch in diameter and was a collection of letters spelling out an acronym that had no meaning to Aubrey or the Google Search engine that read: *POTM*.

Aubrey handed Alex the phone and she recognized it instantly, "That's one of the "Professional of the Month" pins that they used to give out!" She brought the phone closer to her and squinted at the picture on the screen, "But this one looks different, like it's a different font from what I've seen. The one I got last year before they ran out and had to stop the ritual was written in your basic Times New Roman font while this one has Italic lettering. It might have belonged to Sean, but I never saw him wearing one before. A lot of the managers who have them use them as tie pins, but Sean never did. He had a golf club one."

Well that's something. At least I know what the dumb thing stands for now and that the person it belonged to had to have worked there for at least two years, Aubrey thought to himself as he took back his phone and once more placed it in his pocket.

Again there was a silence between the two of them, but this time it was filled with the formation of thoughts and the eagerness to share them.

"You know, all the news feeds I read said his body was found under boxes in the freezer, like maybe Sean had some sort of accident, bumped his head, became unconscious, and then froze to death. Did you guys figure out where he hit his head? I mean, on what did he hit it?"

"Why do you ask?"

"Well maybe, since we think person X may have been the one to kill him, whether an accident or no, maybe the assault to the head happened back near his desk instead of in the freezer. Sean was working on something when I left him. He may have opened the back door and returned to his desk or he may have been attacked while on his way back there. There's a lot of metal shelving in the back to store stuff on like wine bottles and other grocery items. The floor itself is basically evil incarnate."

"The floor?"

"It's pure cement and very unforgiving! Just last month Marty from meat department tripped on the floor mats and broke his arm when he landed on it."

*Why didn't I think of that! They said there should have been some blood or skin matter left behind! We never thoroughly checked the area around his desk for signs of struggle—the store is a forensics' nightmare, what with all the people coming and going—and it was just too big to search everywhere with just the aid of our tiny unit, especially for something not deemed a true murder. If it had been dubbed a sure homicide, then I probably could have gotten Helmer to call in a Milwaukee team and they would have torn through that place, and might have—*Aubrey suddenly stood up. He fished out some bills—enough to pay for both Alex's drink and his untouched shot—and threw them to the counter. "Thanks for all your help!"

Alex followed him with her eyes, confused by his sudden leave. "Where are you going?"

He smiled a full smile, "You just gave me an idea," was his mysterious response before he made his way to the door. But before exiting he paused and turned back, "Do you work tomorrow?" he asked.

Alex nodded, "I'll be in around eleven."

Aubrey gave a slight head bow in acknowledgement before turning and heading out.

Alex took her time finishing her drink. "That man is weird. I can't believe he paid for my drink and never even touched his! Normally I'd say that was alcohol abuse, but under the circumstances I'm a little proud of him."

Chapter 18

Aubrey left *The Bitter End* no longer bitter and made a detour to the station to pick up something before continuing to chase after his new, nagging string of thought. As he passed his desk on the way to tech storage he noticed a few pictures of Freddy taped to his computer screen as well as a list of phone numbers for available exterminators, but didn't take the time to be offended by them. Captain Helmer didn't see Aubrey enter the building, but tried to catch him while he was on his way out. The Captain's voice was loud and demanding, but Aubrey pretended not to hear his name being called amongst the other busy noises of the precinct and kept on walking.

He drove back to Forestgrove Grocery. As he neared the store he noticed that the front parking lot was still very full, meaning that the chocolate event must still be going on. He hoped Nate's attention would be distracted by all of the customers milling about. Luckily, Aubrey had no intention of finding a parking spot here, and directed his truck toward the unmarked service road leading to the back of the building. Here he found the grocery store's delivery vans parked to one side, flanked by a large black truck and medium sized sports car. The rest of the lot was empty, save for the dumpsters and the bench in the reserved smoking area.

He pulled into a vacant parking space and turned the engine off, but did not exit his vehicle right away. Instead, he sat still for awhile trying to enter into the state of mind that person X must have been in on the night Sean was killed.

Why am I parking in back?

To stay out of sight of the camera's and anyone who might be exiting the front of the store. To be closer to where Sean must be because his car is still parked back here.

What am I here to talk to Sean about? What emotions am I feeling? Am I calm? Did I return just because I forgot something?

Maybe, but then why and how did Sean end up dead?

Am I angry?

No—if I was angry I would have come straight in from the front and not taken the time to care if I was seen or not.

Then why am I in the back? Why am I hiding?

Because I'm being cautious. I'm being careful in case something happens, or because something will happen. . .

Aubrey shivered slightly. Cautiousness, nervousness and maybe even a little bit of fear were the signs of a dangerous animal. Happiness, depression, and anger are definite feelings that lead to definite reactions. But cautiousness and fear are different. They are vague and wavering, and can easily turn into something else at a moments notice, with only a little push of direction.

Why am I cautious? Afraid?

Because of Sean or of something that he did/said/will do.

"Motive really is everything, isn't it?" Aubrey said aloud to himself as he sighed and opened his door, the forensic kit he borrowed clutched tightly in his hand.

When he reached the back door he found that it was still unlocked and was somewhat relieved that he didn't have to ring the bell and draw attention to himself. After letting himself in he looked around to find himself in the big Receiving Area. Directly ahead of him was the set of double doors that let to the sales floor; through their windows he could see lots of people strolling around the aisles. To his left was a door that led to the meat department, and a second one that led to an electrical room. On his right was an entrance to the deli kitchen and the hallway that led to the desks of the managers. The lighting here was only about half as bright as that on the grocery floor, and shadows were abundant amongst the bloated U-boats and grocery carts piled high with back up or expired goods. Aubrey noticed how his steps echoed slightly as he made his way toward Sean's desk, confirming to himself that sneaking up on Sean wasn't an impossibility, but improbable unless you knew the territory well, or had quieter shoes.

He reached Sean's old desk and noticed that it had been stripped bare since his visit just yesterday—the family pictures and product posters had all been taken away. January's sheet had been ripped from the desk calendar and the blank dates of February shone a brilliant white. Aubrey set down the forensic kit on the desk and turned to the computer. Curiously, he bent closer, shook the mouse to make the log-in screen appear, and was annoyed to find that Sean's login and password no longer worked. "Someone trying to erase him, huh?"

Aubrey left the computer alone and opened up the kit. It held all the basics one might need for evidence gathering including a handheld Luminol H_2O_2 spray, which Aubrey plucked gingerly from its contents. Starting with the areas around the desk, he began spraying a thin layer of the chemical spray in hopes of finding a trace of blood that might confirm Alex's suspicion. Luminol is a brilliant tool which reacts with any iron it encounters, including that found in the hemoglobin part of a bloodstain, turning the sprayed, stained area into a fluorescent glow. Even though the supposed murder happened days ago, the spray should be able to find trace elements of iron—unless someone went to a lot of extra work to cleaning up the impact spot.

The floor around the desk was, unfortunately, clean. But Aubrey wasn't going to let go of his suspicions so easily. He slowly walked back toward the rear exit, spraying the spray at random intervals as he went. About ten paces away from where this back hallway and the Receiving floor connected, close to the loading dock doors, Aubrey found what he was looking for. Crouching down with a grin on his face, he tried to get a better look at the blotchy stain that the Luminol spray had revealed. Spraying a few squirts more he discovered that the stain was huge! It might not be blood as he had hoped to find, scrubbed away in vain, but the remains of bleach—a lot of it.

Bending closer to the floor and taking a big whiff, underneath the odor of dirt tracked by dirty shoes, he surely smelled the chlorine-like tang that only bleach has. "So this guy, whoever he is, isn't a total idiot then. What a sloppy job, though."

Aubrey took a couple of quick pictures with his phone and made a mental note to ask Alex if any of the departments used bleach for cleaning, then proceeded to check the empty U-boats in the area for any likewise trace of blood or bleach. *If Sean were injured here, there's no other way to easily move that man's body to the freezer. Person X must have used one of these things.*

Aubrey's examination was interrupted by a body suddenly bursting through the double doors and a meanly uttered, "What are you doing back here?"

Aubrey straightened up and turned to find Parker glaring at him with arms folded across his chest. "I'm detecting things. That what detectives do, right?"

"Normally yeah, but ones that are kicked off of cases generally don't. They just get escorted off the property."

"Is that so?"

Parker took a step forward, "You heard me, buddy. Now get out of here before I do just that."

Aubrey wanted to argue, but figured that might lead somewhere he didn't need to go, "That's news to me. . . Alright, just let me get my things."

Parker nodded and followed Aubrey back to Sean's desk, watching him closely as he put the spray back into its designated spot. Snapping the lid in place Aubrey said, "You guys sure cleaned out Sean's desk quick enough. New person already hired to take over his position?"

"Yeah, Nate gave the position to me."

Aubrey paused, "That's convenient then, isn't it? Going to hire your girlfriend back?"

Parker's fingers hardened into fists, "Do I need to call security?"

"Nope, I'm done for now. How long have you worked here, by the way?"

"Seven years, why?"

"Were you ever deemed a 'Professional of the Month?' "

Parker scowled, "This might come as a shocker to you, but once or twice, yeah. Again, why?"

"Just curious. Congratulations on your promotion," Aubrey tipped his head before making his way back to his truck.

Chapter 19

Aubrey found himself seated in his commandant's office quickly after he left the grocery store. Captain Helmer was not happy as was evident by his hard pacing steps that made the knickknacks on his office bookshelves jiggle slightly with each purposeful stride. Suddenly, Helmer couldn't keep his silence anymore and turned on Aubrey, both hands placed firmly on his oak desk, as he demanded, "What were you doing that would make so many people damn you to hell? I've had several nagging phone calls, a widow wondering when her husband's death investigation will be over, so he can officially be 'laid to rest,' two threats of lawsuits, and the grocery store's actual lawyer from Wayworth Law Offices call to complain about your conduct within the last three days! Aubrey, I understand that this detective stuff is somewhat new for you, but with all of your smarts between the academy and the university you went to, and excellent records in the field, I expected a lot better of you!"

"Sir, I can explain."

"Of course you can. You at least seem to have a method behind your madness. And I appreciate that, but this time your explanations won't cut it. You should have heard that store manager—Mr. Bartley—cursing your name and ancestry! You really couldn't have waited to call in the tip about the meat manager until after his little soirée? The guy wasn't going anywhere. And what exactly happened this morning? All I heard was there was this giant weasel with ketchup—you know what, never mind. It doesn't matter. I guess your main problem is that you're young—you only see the right and wrong of a situation. You forget that there are always politics behind a thing and you need to play by those rules too!"

"So I shouldn't have told Hanks that I found his lobster thief?"

"That's another thing—Hanks told me you recognized the guy from a couple of your trips to various Sheboygan drinking fountains. You don't have a drinking problem, now, do you? I understand what happened to your cousin down in Milwaukee was probably a huge shock to your system, but no man on my team lets his emotional problems get in the way of his work, do you hear me?!"

"I hear you. But what about my case?"

"What case? You've been pulled from that case. I'm now debating if I should have you temporarily put on leave for behavioral issues."

"But sir, you can't do that! Not now! I just found evidence that Sean probably was murdered! There was bleach all over the hallway near his desk, probably used to cover up Sean's blood and I have a witness that claims he had a late night visitor—"

"Listen. It's a grocery store. It probably uses bleach to clean up lots of spills, for all we know—gets rid of wine stains when someone breaks a bottle. I have a couple of your 'suspects,' including a grieving widow, threatening to sue for harassment. I have an angry store manager that's saying you're stressing his employees and preventing the place from making any sort of revenue. I've looked over your reports thus far, which are anorexic at best by the way, and there's no proof that this was a murder. This thing was an accidental death as far as I can tell and I want you to close this case before the headache you're causing escalates to the higher-ups, or worse, the press."

"Captain, my gut is telling me that there's more to this case."

Helmer looked at Aubrey, disappointment clearly written on his face. Giving a deep sigh he said, "That's exactly what your father used to say back when he and I worked together. He and I were partners for a long time." Helmer shook his head as if trying to keep the memories at bay, then said, "So you have a gut feeling. Alright, here's what I'll do. You ponder over your findings so far and if you can give me anything by tomorrow afternoon that can solidly prove this a murder I'll keep the case open. But, I'm putting some other hound to lead the pack after the scent—you can take a secondary seat on this one due to your conduct. And if you can't find anything concrete, then I'm stamping this one as 'closed' and you can type up your final report and put it on my desk come Tuesday morning. Now get out of my office and find where your gut feelings are coming from—and if they take you to the end of a bottle and I find out then I'm kicking you off my team. Got it?"

Aubrey shut the door quietly after he left the office. The people who had desks close by tried to keep their curious glances a secret, but he caught them sneaking peeks just the same as he passed. *They probably heard the whole conversation. So I have until tomorrow afternoon then, huh?* Aubrey snorted, *Bless the old man for leaving such a strong impression with his old work buddies.* "However this plays out, I'll have to give him a call and thank him."

Chapter 20

Aubrey didn't waste much time. Once he reached his apartment he grabbed a bunch of loose leaf paper, a permanent marker, and a bunch of thumb tacks that he kept handy and arranged them on the card table in his dinning room. He appreciated technology, but always found himself falling back on old school pen and paper whenever he had a serous issue to sort out, as if making the problem tangible would make the solution easier to reach. He then took a few minutes to decide what music he wanted to use as background noise and settled on a Pandora station that played music from the 60's and 70's. A Simon and Garfunkel classic came on a few seconds later, and Aubrey turned his thoughts from *The Sounds of Silence* to focus totally on the Ritter case.

He started by writing **Sean** at the top of one of the pieces of paper and then writing the key facts he had found out about the guy underneath:

- Ex-military

- Gaining a MA in Management

- Has two kids

- Interested in younger women

- Generally disliked by everyone

Aubrey finished writing and tacked the piece of paper into the center of one of his blank living room walls. He continued writing various cards and tacking them to the same wall until eventually he had a collage of organized information staring back at him. He divided the cards by possible motives, and listed all of the possible suspects underneath. It was interesting how many of these names appeared more than once.

Under the heading **Having Sex with a Co-worker/Underling** was written the names of Sean's wife, Parker, Cyndi/Evan (at least now he knew why Cyndi had been so shifty the first time he had talked to her—she was trying to keep her relationship a secret), and the various cute girls that worked behind the counters.

Under **Dictatorship-like Attitude (or being an a-hole)** he had put down the names of Larry (from the kitchen), coffee shop ladies (apparently there were rumors of the grocery store buying out the coffee shop and that if that happened Sean would be put in charge of it), Evan (currently detained), and Parker.

Under **Possible Discovery of Thievery** was Evan (currently detained), Julie, and Tim (the peacock). He had also added a small blurb which he circled, "Where is the missing $500????"

And under **Random Grudges** was written ex-military buddies (???) as well as the names of Parker (for drug abuse?), Claire (for making her do his job), Julie (the Work Wife), and Daniel (for his religious views).

He added a new sheet which read **POTM (Professional of the Month)** and tacked it away from the other papers. He added the following details to the bottom of that page:

- Found near the body

- Has to belong to someone who has worked there for more than two years

- Normally <u>not</u> worn by the deceased

- Fell off murderer while arranging the victim's body???

Looking over the wall he reviewed his work so far. There was a spider web alright, with a few connections between the parts, but all of this he already knew. He needed to figure out something new, something that would paint a bigger picture.

"They sure deleted his work account pretty fast, didn't they? I wonder who ordered it? Nate, maybe. Or it's some sort of company procedure. . ." He walked back to the table and from his notebook took out the collection of folded e-mails he had printed out the day before.

There were a few invoices that Sean had to finalize, a proposal from a possible new cheese vendor looking to sell their product there, and as Aubrey shifted through the plethora of catering orders for the following morning (that didn't get filled for obvious reasons), a letter of welcome fell out and fluttered to the floor. Picking it up, he read, "Looking forward to working with you in the future!" It was from a Ronald Wayworth.

Aubrey paused and reread that last entry. "Ronald Wayworth. Could he be. . .?"

Aubrey let the question hang in the air as he drew out his phone and brought up his Google App. In the search engine he typed in the name and waited to see what results might be displayed. To his delight, the very first one was a link to the profile page of a Ronald Wayworth of Wayworth Law Offices located in Sheboygan, WI. "Now why would the store's lawyer be looking forward to working with Sean in the future? Was he going to be promoted? Start up his own business? Or maybe he was protecting himself from a threat of some sort of law suit?"

Aubrey ran his hands through his hair. *Hotel California* was in mid-play and he mouthed the words to himself as he decided to take a short break, and headed into the kitchen. He paused with his hand on the handle of the fridge. *The only thing in here is beer*, he reminded himself. He swallowed the dry lump in his throat. God was he thirsty! And now that he was aware of his thirst he also became aware of how shaky his hands were and how there was a pressure behind his eyes like the beginnings of a headache. *How long has it been since my last drink? I never did drink that shot. I had those samples around lunch time. That was only about five hours ago and I'm showing signs of withdrawal? Shit!*

Aubrey slammed a fist into the counter top, his breathing coming heavily. For a moment his mind was in a state of panic—battling between an ego that believed nothing could enslave it and the reality that he was using liquor to dull his aches, a fact only he seemed to be blind to.

You could stop at anytime—right now. Or tomorrow. You aren't hooked. Just have one more.

But you heard what Helmer said. . .

Who cares? This is your house, your money, your time to relax. You're technically off the clock.

But the case. . .

Might be clearer after you've had a few. Besides you won't be able to think once the withdrawal symptoms worsen.

Suddenly Aubrey straitened up. He had made his decision.

He opened the fridge and took out the three remaining bottles. They were cold in his hands as he went in search of his bottle opener. When he couldn't find where he left it he almost panicked again but thought up a solution to his problem. With extreme force he took the bottles and threw them as hard as he could into the kitchen sink, shattering them into a multitude of pieces. One shard ricocheted off the side of the sink and embedded itself into Aubrey's hand. He pulled it out slowly, unfeeling of the pain as he watched the liquid slosh noisily down the drain in a whirlpool like motion.

Again he tried to swallow the lump which seemed glued to the back of his throat. Then, being careful of the glass now sitting in his sink, he rinsed off his injured hand and dried it with a paper towel. It was a superficial cut and stopped bleeding rather quickly. That done, he pulled forward the ancient coffee pot from the dark corner it had been shoved into. Besides the toaster this was his only counter appliance.

After a few minutes of listening to the sputtering and hissing he poured himself his first cup of Joe and walked back to take a gander at the evidence laid out before him, fearful how the night might go, but determined to get through it just the same.

Chapter 21

The next day was Sunday, February 13th and while there weren't any special events at the store, Forestgrove Grocery was just as crazy as it had been the day before. The threat of the oncoming storm wasn't just rearranging the plans of hundreds of lovers, making them celebrate their relationships a day early—it was also causing the type of panic where all the milk, bread, and toilet paper disappear in an instant.

Back behind the deli counter yet again, Alex laughed to herself as she said aloud, "I hope this is another one of the weatherman's false predictions. I'd die laughing if tomorrow the sun was shinning and the temperature was in the forties." It was in the early afternoon with only Jacquelyn and herself to man the fort, and luckily for them most people didn't consider sliced meat to be up to par with tenderloin and prime rib, so their department wasn't being harassed by vultures like the harried meat department.

Jacquelyn chided her, "You really need to start watching the weather. They're saying that what's coming our way is going to be the storm of the season! An ice storm for the ages!"

"Nah, I prefer to just look out the window to see what it's doing and then keep my car supplied in case of an emergency. I have blankets and a candle in a tin can for heat. I also have a shovel that I toss in the back seat at the first snowfall of the season."

Jacquelyn just shook her head, "You're hopeless, you know that? No internet, you don't watch the weather. I'm surprised you even have a cell phone!" Changing the topic, she added, "I just hate driving in the snow. It's so dangerous!"

Again Alex laughed, "Only because of all the idiots who don't know how to drive in it! Personally I love it! I plug in my heavy metal music and shout: *Bring it on, Mother Nature!*"

Jacquelyn chortled, "I could see you doing that!"

They were silent for a time and Alex's thoughts became distracted. She still hadn't seen the detective yet today and he hadn't been in the coffee shop either. With the way Nate was walking around, still grumbling about the arrest and some other thing—a prank?—that happened yesterday, Alex had a feeling that not only was Aubrey no longer welcome here, but that he might be purposely bared from entering the store without the aid of a warrant. She found herself greatly disappointed at this possible fact.

Her thoughts were also troubled because Cyndi hadn't shown up to work her shift in the bakery that morning. She wasn't returning any of the text messages Alex had sent her either.

"Hello ladies!" a familiar voice suddenly called. Alex's heart skipped a beat.

"Hi Bobby!" Jacquelyn basically swooned. Jacquelyn was closer to the counter, and Alex was going to let her help him this time, but he acknowledged Alex directly.

"Alex, would you mind making me one of your special burger's today? This cold weather is making me crave something spicy."

"Sure, coming right up," she said as she donned a fresh pair of gloves and disappeared in to the kitchen.

Reappearing seven minutes later with Alex's own creation: A Rabid Freddy Burger which consisted of a medium rare piece of meat slathered in hot sauce, covered with pepper jack cheese, grilled onions and jalapeños, bacon, and wedged between a buttered and then toasted bun in a sealed to-go container, Alex waved Bobby back over to the counter and handed him his early dinner/late lunch.

"Oh thank you so much! This looks fantastic. You know, you should be a chef. You'd be very good at it!"

"Maybe in my next life. Have a good day, Bobby."

"You too! Stay warm!"

Alex watched as he pranced away and was startled as once again Aubrey spoke from right beside her, "You should date that guy."

"Damn it! People need to stop sneaking up on me like that! And what is it with everyone telling me that I need to date someone? I am fine on my own. At least for the time being!"

Aubrey shrugged and continuing to lean on the salad case. He looked down into it as he said, "Fair enough, but he obviously likes you."

"That boy is too fair to be single; which means, he is already taken, is a player, or is gay. None of those scenarios work well for me, now do they?"

Aubrey shrugged, "Just saying you could try giving him the time of day. Your GPS looks weird, by the way."

"My what?"

"Your German Potato Salad. Those are red potatoes, right? And you leave the skins on? That's not normally how people around here make it."

"I suppose you would know since 'Steiner' is a German name, right?" Alex asked dryly.

"That and I do cook a little bit."

"Okay, Mr. Picky, would you like to try it before you condemn it?" Alex snatched two black sample cups, one larger than the other by two ounces, from a nearby basket and held them up. "I can give you a sample, or a *sample*. Which would you rather have?"

Aubrey chuckled, "No thanks. I'm not very hungry at the moment. I'll just take your word that it tastes great. I just thought I'd make the comment that it wasn't made in the traditional sense, that's all."

"Yeah, well, that was a Sean decision. Maybe that'll be changing too. We just found out that Parker will be taking over our department, which is annoying because he doesn't know the first thing about cooking or deli service."

Aubrey seemed down as he said, "Yeah, I heard about that."

Alex picked up on the slight change of tone and asked, "Everything alright?"

Aubrey shook his head in response, "Not exactly. I've been told to mark the Ritter case as 'closed' and as an 'accidental death' unless further evidence shows up."

"So you didn't find anything by his desk, like signs of a struggle or something?"

"Oh, but I did. That's why I came by today, to tell you thanks for the tip, but it still wasn't enough to convince my boss that he was murdered."

"What?! That doesn't make any sense!"

"Do any departments use bleach to clean anything?"

Alex thought for a moment, "Yes. The meat department uses it to clean out their seafood case."

"The evidence I found can't be undoubtedly connected with Sean's death. Besides the fact that the bleach stain I found was over a week old and had already been trampled on for some time, making further analysis futile, it also wasn't discovered by his desk, but closer to the Receiving Area. So it could have been a careless meat department associate the whole time. But besides that, you were right about something else."

"I was? About what?"

"I should have tried the honey approach. Bartley threw a fit, called the store's lawyer about possible harassment charges, who in turn called my supervisor." Aubrey shrugged, "So the investigation is over."

"Oh," was all Alex could muster.

"Anyways, I just wanted to tell you that in person. Figured you would rather hear it from me than a newspaper. So, thanks again for the tip. If you think of anything else, don't hesitate to call or shoot me a text. Maybe we can reopen the case, but it seems really unlikely at this point."

" 'Kay."

Before things could get anymore awkward, Aubrey took his leave. "See you around."

"Yeah, maybe," was Alex's lame response.

When Alex turned to walk back to the prep table she

found Jacquelyn glaring at her.

"What?" she asked.

Jacquelyn was shaking her head as she scolded, "First of all, I wish I had your boy problems. You're like a walking magnet for the hotties!"

"You mean a magnet for the unavailable."

"And secondly, *that* was how you said goodbye: "Yeah, maybe?" I expected better of you, missy. At least you have his number—"

"Jacquelyn. . ."

"He's the one who suggested that you 'shoot him a text!' "

"Just stop, please!"

"Fine. But I'm very disappointed."

"Okay. Got it. Can we get back to work now?" But even though her bravado was showing, Alex felt a little depressed about the outcome of the whole situation. She supposed she should be happy that there wasn't any evidence of murder—after all that would mean she was working alongside a killer. But she was kind of bummed that with the case being over, she wouldn't be able to talk to Aubrey anymore. He seemed like an interesting guy.

Alex shrugged to herself, *You have enough interesting stuff going on in your life as it is. You don't need to chase after more.* But this time her advice sounded lame even to her.

Chapter 22

Unfortunately for Alex, the weather man had been correct in his predictions. The day before had been in the forties and sunny, letting the top layer of snow melt to slush and as the night continued rain started to fall, which as the temperature dropped, turned to ice. By morning a thin layer of the slippery substance covered the majority of the roadways, but the precipitation hadn't ended. It continued, now as large heavy snow flakes which masked the ice in a lovely coat of glittering white.

When snow hazards happen in other states not located in the Midwest region, schools cancel classes, businesses close, production lines shut down—whole cities become eerie ghost towns for the day because they don't have the equipment to handle such miserable gifts from above. But in the Midwest, especially around Sheboygan, Wisconsin, everyone carries on as if their cars weren't being bombarded by demon fighter pilots disguised as chunks of ice. People still take quick trips to Walmart or to go buy cigarettes at corner gas stations, schools never cancel, and unless it really is that bad of a storm, businesses keep on staying busy.

With a mug of coffee in hand, Alex stared out the window of her apartment for a few seconds and then shrugged, "I think I'll leave a little earlier just to make sure I'm not late."

Her mood that morning was not the greatest. She felt down and depressed, probably due to the fact that the Ritter case was officially closed and her short time with Aubrey was probably over for good. *It's not like I wanted to date him or anything*, she told herself, *it's just that he was a cool guy and I would have liked to hang out with him some more.* It also was a little unnerving that Sean's killer hadn't been brought to justice. *Maybe it was just a fluke accident after all. There wasn't any real evidence pointed to foul play.*

Alex's mood darkened further when she opened her garage door and discovered a large snow drift blocking the exit. Sighing, she removed the shovel from her backseat and began to clear a path. She had to stop two more times to shovel away monstrous drifts just to get out of her apartment complex, and for a moment debated whether or not she should call in for the day. With curse words flying under her breath she pointed out to herself that the plowing company normally didn't get to the apartment parking lots until almost noon on days like today and that probably once she made it to an actual road, the going would be smoother—even with the strong north wind and the heavy flakes that battered against the windshield like an angry hornet's nest. In the end, stubbornness and determination won out and she forced her way out of the parking lot and onto a recently plowed city street.

"See, this will be a piece of cake!" She exclaimed in triumph.

What normally took her ten minutes to drive into work turned into almost fifty. During this time she only fishtailed a tiny bit at the first intersection near her apartment, stopping too suddenly for a red light. Once she reached the highway, after the fourth car she saw in the ditch she almost turned back again, thinking her quest a sure suicide. However, even with the wind violently leaning on her car, the snake-like tendrils of drifting snow weaving between her tires, and the fresh flakes swirling down, looking like she was part of a light speed adventure—and therefore being forced to move at a mere thirty miles an hour—she didn't want to turn around. If she pulled onto a turnaround or a side road, then she would definitely get stuck and sitting around for God knew how long for a tow truck wasn't an enticing option. So instead, with both hands tightly clasping the wheel, she crawled toward Forestgrove Grocery, letting the idiots zoom pass her, while screaming along to the cranked up music of her *The Used* collection to keep her panic at bay.

She was so happy to see her destination looming just up ahead, but frowned at the final obstacle placed in front of it—a totally unplowed side road. With her face set she gunned the engine and jerked the wheel, giving just enough power and direction to make it over the foot-tall wall of snow chunks pushed together by a merciless plow, and then immediately she lifted her foot from the pedals on the floor, keeping it hovered above the brake. The car surged over the hindrance and began to squirm as the tires searched for purchase. She almost did a 180, before the wheels eventually found traction and she was once again able to force the car to go in the correct lane.

Thanking the heavens that there were no other cars about, she parked as well as she could without being able to see the lines (because they were totally obliterated by white), turned the engine off, and took a moment to compose herself. She didn't mind driving in snow, but that had been a horror she hoped to never repeat.

Grabbing her bag she high-tailed it to the store. This was not a nice snowstorm—one that's so quiet you can hear the flakes hit the earth with a gentle crunch—but one where you might think that Mother Nature is out for revenge with savage howls from the wind, trees swaying and bending violently, and snow that's more ice than flake which bites and claws at everything it can reach. Alex was eager to get inside and escape it.

She went to the coffee shop hoping to get something

that might thaw her nerves as well as her being. But when she entered the shop, a nervous Jennifer called over one shoulder, "I'm sorry dear, but we're closing up shortly."

"What?" Alex asked between labored breaths.

Jen turned, "Oh, hello Alex. This storm is something else! Did you make it here alright? How many people were in the ditch?"

Alex stamped her boots off at the door before entering the shop further. "That was an adventure. Maybe six, seven? So you guys are closing for the day?"

Jen nodded sadly as she explained, "I was able to get to work because I only live a few blocks from here, but I'm this close to having a panic attack. I just can't stand being in here and watching it come down—I feel like I'm getting buried alive! Here," she said, handing over a large to go container, "this one's on the house. It's the only stuff I haven't dumped yet. I already called my boss and he agrees that it's better to close shop today. It's supposed to be all ice soon—the largest storm since the eighties, or something like that! I normally don't mind snowstorms, but this one is ridiculous!"

Alex took the offered cup and frowned at it.

"Will you be alright getting home? If you need to you can stay at my place tonight."

Alex gave a weak smile, "That's very kind of you. I'll see what happens and let you know later."

As she left the coffee shop to enter the grocery store she paused and took a quick look around. With all of the snow everywhere—flying through the air, being pushed into corners of buildings, and layering the ground like a batch of vanilla frosting—you would never think that spring was supposed to be only one month away. Like the bite of a snapping turtle, winter just didn't want to let go.

What a wonderful Valentine's Day, she thought to herself miserably.

Chapter 23

Alex really should have called in for the day.

It was around nine-thirty in the a.m. when she arrived at work, two hours before her scheduled shift was supposed to begin, but when she circled around to the deli to see who had made it in, she found a lonely Claire working by herself, scurrying around like a hyper squirrel. While there had been no one in the coffee shop, there were a few people meandering through the store, some of whom had ordered breakfast and were now casually waiting for it to be done.

"Hey, Alex!" Claire called, "Could you start right away? I'm by myself right now and—"

"Yeah, just let me clock in quick."

Putting on her apron, Alex listened as Claire relayed to her the orders that needed to be completed yet for catering. "We're still doing that today? Is anyone here to deliver this stuff?" Alex asked.

But Claire only shook her head, "I'll explain in a second. I need to flip the eggs—I'll be right back."

Sighing, Alex turned to the prep counter and began making side salads as instructed.

After a few minutes Claire reappeared with three plates full of steaming eggs, bacon, and potatoes and delivered them to the small group leaning on the counter. With a smile she wished them to all have a good day, but as thcy left and she turned back to Alex her smile vanished.

"The people at the offices across the way who actually made it in to work 'don't feel like walking over here for lunch' so they ordered this large array of sandwiches and things to be delivered. I already have the drinks and bags of chips gathered."

"Sure, but who's going to deliver it?"

"Nate, I guess, because everyone else called in."

"But doesn't Emily live, like, five minutes away?"

Claire rolled her eyes in response, "I'm so happy you're here. I was going to call you and ask if you were going to make it in or not, but then all these people came in for breakfast—"

"On a day like today? Really?!"

"Yes! They're coming in on snow mobiles—and one family came in by sleigh! Can you believe that?"

"Wow. So Nate's delivering then?"

"Yes. He's out in his truck right now picking up someone from meat department because otherwise there's no one to cover the department. I was afraid I was going to have to stay here all day by myself!"

Jeez, this is crazy! Alex thought to herself. "We shouldn't even be open today. . ."

"I agree, but since we're here, might as well get something done, right?"

Alex hadn't actually worked alongside Claire for quite some time. Sure, their paths often crossed during shift change and they did relay various messages back and forth with each   other, but they hadn't had any time to really talk, vent, or gossip like in the weeks when Alex first started.

There was a slightly awkward silence for awhile, but

soon enough general questions were asked about each other's families, cats, what books they were currently reading, etc..

Finally, Alex couldn't stand not knowing any longer and asked, "So, Claire, why didn't you take Sean's job?"

Claire didn't answer right away. Then slowly she said, "I could have taken the coordinator position, and I know I would have been good at it, since Sean was basically making me do his job to begin with; but honestly, I don't want it. Harry and I are trying to start a family and when it comes down to it, being there for my family is way more important to me than my job. And Sean had to be here all the time to finish paperwork, to supervise—that's not the right lifestyle for me."

Alex nodded, "I guess I could understand that. However, I would rather work under you than Parker. He's a cool enough guy, but does he honestly know what he's doing over here?"

Claire laughed, "I had to show him around and he had no idea where anything was or that we even have our own little walk-in cooler in the kitchen!"

"Wow. Guess we're going to have some fun times ahead of us then, huh?"

Claire smiled, "I guess so. We'll just have to wait and see what happens."

~*~*~*~*~

The feeling of anticipation and the strain of urgency was a tangible thing to the few employees of Forestgrove Grocery who made it into work that February day; anticipation to see how bad it would get outside, and the urgency to escape the storm and the boredom, as well as the desire to return to the safety of their burrows.

But time continued to drag, the hours to crawl, the minutes to hesitate, the seconds barely measurable. Eventually Alex was left alone to man the deli. Besides her, only four others (Nate in his office, Pat in the meat department, Daniel the bagger leisurely cleaning miscellaneous things, and Tim at the courtesy desk) could be counted, kept separated by aisles and isolated by counters of glass. The store's internet connection was affected by the harsh weather—causing the radio station to cut in and out unexpectedly; the sudden silences adding an eerie effect to the entire place.

Alex sang songs quietly to herself to help ease some of the anxiety she was feeling; comfort songs like *Me and Bobby McGee* and Harry Chapin classics. It was about four-thirty, when she was in the middle of making take and bake pizzas—laying out the cardboard bottoms, the different thicknesses of crusts, swirling on the tomato sauce, sprinkling the cheese, and layering the toppings—when the power went out.

The instant blackness was so startling that Alex dropped the container of pizza sauce. She heard the contents splatter all over the floor, including a large glob which landed on her shoes. With the sun already blocked by storm clouds, the windows on the far wall provided no assistance, and for a second Alex felt fear starting to surface. Pat from the meat department let out a startled scream and somewhere amongst the grocery aisles a loud f-bomb was dropped.

While Alex started fumbling through her pockets to try to find her cell phone, there was an abruptly loud clicking noise followed by a low humming, signaling the back up generator kicking in. A few seconds later the orange glow of emergency lights radiated above the various doorways and wall coolers. They didn't make the store bright as day, but they gave enough light to make movement possible without running into any blunt objects.

Visions of vengeful ghosts and a warning of bad fortune suddenly flashed before Alex's eyes and she had to shake her head to clear it all away. *Get a hold of yourself. It's just the weather!* Swallowing the lump that had formed in her throat Alex shouted, "You okay over there, Patty?"

The other lady laughed nervously, "Yes, I'm fine. Just got a little spooked there for a second."

Nate's bustle came swiftly from the shadows and asked, "Everyone alright?"

"We're both fine back here," Alex responded but then looked at the mess at her feet. "A little messy, but alright."

Nate nodded, "Damn this weather! Alright, I'm calling it quits for today for all of us! Shut down your departments, and let's head out. Pat, Tim agreed to give you a ride home since you both live in the same direction. And ladies, don't worry too much about cleaning up."

"What should I do about my half-finished pizzas?" Alex asked more to herself then the people at ears length. *I can't wrap them if the saran wrap machine isn't working.*

"Just put them in the cooler or something," Nate retorted. Alex watched as he ran his hands violently over his balding head. He was clearly irritated. "Damn it. This back up system is so damn old—I hope it will keep the freezers working. Otherwise. . . all of that product! Wasted!"

Alex heard the grief and anger clearly in Nate's wavering tone, and trying to take away some of his worry she asked, "Isn't there someone you can call to come—"

But Nate snapped away her assistance, "Just clean up your shit and get out of here! I'm the manager and I'll handle this!"

Even though there was a glass case and about fifty yards distance between herself and Nate, his venomous words made her physically flinch by their crudeness. She had never heard him swear before.

"O-okay," she replied meekly, but Nate had already spun on a heel and retreated back into the shadows that led to the front of the store.

Chapter 24

Aubrey glared at the clock stationed above Helmer's empty office. It read 4:40. *I wish I could call in just because of a little ice and snow*, he growled to himself. *But I get to finish this damn report by tomorrow.*

He wasn't crabby because of the withdrawal effects of his alcoholism—those had passed for the most part in the wee hours of the morning. He had stopped shaking the afternoon before and the headaches had disappeared with the second cup of stale coffee from the policeman's lounge earlier this morning when he had first clocked in. No, he wasn't crabby because he wanted a drink. He was crabby because he was cold, the heater here in HQ seeming to be only a myth, because the jokes about rodent infestations were starting to get old, and because he was basically stir-crazy from being at his desk all day. Helmer had been right, he hadn't been keeping up with his logs for the different stages of his (now closed) investigation and playing catch up was a pain in the ass.

Joseph (Joey) Hanks, one of the other detectives of the unit came up to Aubrey's cluttered desk and asked, "This weather is ridiculous, isn't it!? I'm kind of glad you caught my lobster thief for me so I had an excuse to stay indoors! Normally paperwork is a bitch, but on a day like today. . ."

Aubrey shrugged and leaned back in his swivel chair, "I see what you're saying." He looked at all of the vacant seats around him and frowned. *This is a tad better then responding to ditch calls like all these other suckers, and at least I'm making some overtime.* He turned his attention back to Hanks and noticed how he was sporting his civilian winter coat. "So are you heading out for the night? Not on call then, you lucky dog?"

Joey laughed, "Thank God, I'm not! The little woman back home has already called me three times to inform me how much snow there is piled up in front of the house. It'll be a miracle if I can even make it into the driveway! Besides it's Valentine's Day and you know how women are—on a night like tonight they'll want to snuggle with some hot chocolate and stuff like that."

Aubrey picked up the childlike gleam in Joey's eye and said suggestively, "Snuggling—so that's what you call it, huh?"

Joey laughed some more as he wished Aubrey a good night and turned to leave, but then paused as if he suddenly remembered something. "Oh yeah, a little detail you might want to add to your report: now I know it might not lead to anything concrete, but when my men searched through Evan Sanderson's desk drawers we found an envelope hidden under a stock pile of old paperwork housing $500. We assumed it was the amount missing from the safe, but when I was interrogating the guy, he swore that the money wasn't his and that he didn't steal it either. He claimed it was planted in the desk drawer and that he had no idea it was there until we told him about it." Joey shrugged at Aubrey's perplexed expression, "Of course he was probably lying. Just thought you might like to know. Have a good night. Drive safe!"

After detective Hanks' exit, Aubrey stared at his computer screen where the words of his report stared back at him impassively. *So the $500 had been found after the search of the seafood manager's desk area*, he thought to himself. Then aloud he added, "Strange that the $500 didn't turn up during our initial sweep. Stranger still that Evan would admit to stealing fish and other things, but not a load of cash."

When his desk phone jangled to life, Aubrey was barely able to keep himself from jumping. Chuckling at himself, he picked up the receiver on the second ring. The drawling voice of Courtney, the station's head secretary came through in its usually lazy way, "Detective Steiner? You have a call for you—coming all the way from Mexico," (she pronounced it Meh-He-Co with an extra nasally flare). "Sending it through now. . ."

There was a small click as Courtney transferred the call—the signal for Aubrey to introduce himself which he did in a smooth two lines, "Good evening, you've reached Detective Steiner of the Sheboygan Country Police Department. How may I help you?"

The voice from the other end stuttered a few times, but otherwise was incoherent. Aubrey's eyebrows drew together as he remembered this call was coming from Mexico. He didn't know anyone south of the boarder, and with the storm outside he wondered if the long distance connection would hold. There was a pause from the stuttering and then the voice tried again—this time coming in clear, "Detective Steiner is it? This here is Victor Clivedale. . . I'm the one who pays the bills for Forestgrove Grocery. They tell me you're the one heading the investigation—"

A high-pitched woman's voice suddenly cut in and shouted into the speaker making Aubrey have to pull the phone away from his ear in order to prevent permanent damage. Shrilly she asked, "How is Edith doing, the ex-Mrs. Ritter? It's positively terrible, what happened!"

"Henrietta, get off the phone! This is man's business!" Aubrey thought he could hear Mrs. Clivedale's pout even with the thousands of miles between the two phones. A moment later it was just the two guys talking again with the ball in Mr. Clivedale's court. "Detective Steiner, I'm calling to let you know we're cutting our vacation early this year and that we are on our way home—it's just that we're stranded at this damn airport! You guys must be having a grand old time up there! Nothing even going close to the Midwest is heading out—"

Aubrey thought it best to interrupt. With an apologetic tone, in the hopes of cooling any fires that Mr. Clivedale was hoping to start, he said, "Yes, Mother Nature must be angry about something. But Mr. Clivedale, if you don't mind me saying, there's no real point in cutting your vacation short—the Ritter case is considered closed. In fact, I'm finishing up the final paperwork right now."

There was a long pause on the other end and Aubrey had a clear vision of Victor relaying the information back to his wife, both of them with satisfied smiles on their faces and their minds already turning back to those ice cold Pina Coladas waiting for them back at the hot, sandy beaches. . . Aubrey wasn't ready for the anger that came bursting out of the receiver instead.

"What the Hell do you mean the Ritter case is 'closed?!' We were just informed about the man's death about four hours ago! I refuse to believe that you could have done a thorough investigation about my store's general manager in such a short time! And without having any requests, questions, or other legal issues sent through us! You must be pulling my leg, son!"

It was Aubrey's turn to be confused, "U-um, Sir. Did you say you just found out about Sean's death today? May I ask who you heard it from?"

"From my lawyer, of course! They sent me a lot of damn paperwork to go along with the phone call too!"

"So you didn't hear about Sean's death about—oh,

say—two weeks ago? Because Nate Bartley said—"

"Did you say Bartley?! That bastard! Why the hell have you been talking to him? That bum was fired last month. He's been stealing money from the store for almost half a year—and the idiot thought I wouldn't notice! I faxed in the pink slip the same day I sent the congratulations letter to Sean for his promotion to Store Manager—now *that* man knows how to get stuff done! I would have been making a 20% higher profit, probably starting to show by June. Don't tell me that bum is still working there, why when I get back up there—"

It was during Mr. Clivedale's rant that the phone started to act funny. At first it cut in and out, went back to making stuttering sounds, and then all of a sudden to a deep silence. "Hello? Mr. Clivedale, are you there? Hey!" Aubrey opened up a second line and punched in a few buttons. When Courtney answered, Aubrey sliced into her introduction and asked, "Hey, I lost that last call. Is there any way to get it back? Did—"

But Courtney wouldn't be ignored, "Listen, you won't be able to get that call back. The caller ID only showed that it was out of country. Besides, I'm busy right now, Aubrey. There's some kind of emergency downtown. I need to direct officers—gotta go!"

Aubrey replaced the phone gently and sat back in his chair. *So Nate was fired a month ago? And Sean was supposed to replace him. . . Maybe he didn't receive the fax. . . But if he did, then he sure had everyone fooled. And in that case I think Mr. Bartley deserves an Oscar for one hell of a performance.*

To himself he added, "And so the domino's start to fall, one by one."

Chapter 25

Back at Forestgrove Grocery, Alex had almost finished putting everything away. All she had left to do was clean up the pizza sauce that painted the floor. There was so much of it that it reminder her of one of those gory crime scenes from the cop drama shows she watched on TV. Some of the minor splatters, like the ones on her shoes and on the sides of the prep table, she was able to wipe clean using towels. Unfortunately for the main spill she would have to go get a mop bucket.

Trudging through the gauntlet of the back alley toward the mop closet was bone-chillingly creepy with the orange lights casting angled shadows in numerous directions. At one point Alex stopped suddenly as she was sure she saw a man hiding in the darker shadows next to the colored printer—and then laughed at her silliness when she realized it was nothing more than the collapsible tent the catering people sometimes used for outside events, all snug and secure in its boxy tote. After that she made it to the mop area with ease, and using the flashlight app on her phone she went to work filling up the bucket. First, a small amount of soap and then water to create a frothy mixture—just enough to cover the mop itself, and then pointed the bucket back toward the deli and the mess to be cleansed.

In the semi-darkness she hadn't realized that she had chosen one of the worst mop buckets until she started to try and move it forward. Two of the wheels on this one were gummed up, making it drive at its best from a side angle, but only at a snail's pace. Frowning, but determined none the less, Alex stuffed her phone back into her pocket and pushed with all her might to get the annoying thing to move.

To herself she said sardonically, "I think I just discovered the next reality television game show! They'll take random people off the street and take them to random places like grocery stores, movie theaters, restaurants—even bowling alleys—and give each contestant a mop bucket. None of them will ever have had access to these buckets before, but each bucket will have some sort of problem—at least one wheel has to be broken. There also will be a regulated amount of water for each person. Then, being timed, each contestant will have to push or pull the bucket through some sort of obstacle course, go through doors, weave through table's maybe, and eventually get to the end where they have this huge mess to clean up! If they slosh water anywhere on the way there then they have to stop and wipe it up. And the first one to clean up the mess with the least amount of time wins the grand prize! How does that sound?"

Alex was too busy announcing her day dream about mop buckets to notice that hers was set on a crash course with a U-boat full of cases of wine. By the time she looked up it was too late and all she was able to do was to jerk the bucket violently toward the center of the aisle, where the resounding effect due to the gummed up wheels was that the bucket stayed mostly stationary while almost two thirds of the contents sloshed over the rim and once again Alex found herself with dirty shoes (well, more clean than dirty since the bucket was full of fresh soapy water). It didn't just end there. The water seemed to be heading out of reach purposely, shooting under the surrounding U-boats and managers desks in thin torrents.

"Today is a fucking nightmare!" Alex shouted, not caring if anyone heard her. She marched back to the mop closet and used her phone again to find a squeegee, brandished it like one might hold a long gun in a military parade, and made her way back toward the accident site.

Luckily for her there was a floor drain close to Sean's

old desk, so with squeegee in hand she began to direct the water that-a-way. She had most of the liquid rounded up and was making a second pass with the squeegee underneath the shelving across the way when she heard the familiar crunch of paper. It was mostly soggy when she pulled it out, but one corner was dry enough to handle. Picking it up, she tried to read what the red letter said in the dim lighting. After reading the first line of it she blinked, then pulled out her phone for a third time, this time not using it as a light, but for its natural purpose.

Back at his desk, Aubrey was checking the Forestgrove Grocery's master schedule he had requested a copy of a few days before—on a day where he assumed that he would still be grilling various grocery people with questions. *Well, you know what they say, that assuming only makes an ass out of you and me.* That's what he had thought earlier this morning when he had begrudgingly taken a seat at his desk and booted up his computer. Now, however, he was grateful that he hadn't simply tossed the thing. *See, it pays to be a pack rat on occasion,* his mind whispered as he scanned the list. It was organized by department, and Nate and all the other big wigs were listed under Administration. Yes, Aubrey saw, Nate did work today, so he could go over there right now and. . .

Aubrey glanced hopefully out of one of the far windows, but the snow was still falling relentlessly. Glancing back at the schedule, Nate was supposed to work the next day also, starting around ten a.m. "Tomorrow will do just as well. It's not like he knows I'm on to him. I just hope Helmer won't blow a gasket when he knows I purposely disobeyed orders again, although under the circumstances I'm sure he'll understand—"

Aubrey was surprised to feel his cell phone vibrating in his pocket. Fishing it out he noted that it was a local, but unknown number, and answered it anyway, "Detective Aubrey Steiner's phone."

He recognized the voice instantly. "Aubrey? This is Alex. I hope you don't mind me calling you randomly like this. . ."

Aubrey smiled, "Of course not. What's up?"

Alex continued, this time in a more rambling fashion, due to nervousness or excitement, Aubrey couldn't quite tell, "Alright, well, I'm at work right now, but we had a blackout and, well, we're closing early and I was cleaning up, but ran the mop bucket into something, and while I was cleaning *that* mess up I found this paper under one of the shelves in the back area near Sean and Parker's desks—it was wedged pretty far back there—and you won't believe me when I tell you what it says! It says: Dear Mr. Bartley, We regret—"

There was suddenly a large *CRACK!* from Alex's end and the line went dead.

"What the hell was that?"

Aubrey checked his phone but the words, *Call Ended* followed by the call timer blinked back at him. He quickly searched through his recent call's listing, selected the last number and hit redial. It rang once and then a recorded message came on, "I'm sorry but the person you are trying to reach is not available. Please hang up and try again later."

Aubrey ended the call but kept his eyes fixed upon the screen. The bad feelings were back again, squirming in his gut like a pocket of restless snakes in a nesting ground— just like the time he went undercover to that crack house last fall. The hopeful, maybe even frightened side of his head said, *Don't worry, she'll call back. This weather really is something, huh?*

"That call wasn't dropped because of the weather," Aubrey said bitterly, standing up and grabbing his coat. He started for the door at a brisk walk which turned quickly into a run. He paused at the reception desk in the hopes of calling backup, but the desk, which was also the call center for emergencies and police communication was busier than an ant hill in fall. There was no time to wait for backup, let alone time to wait patiently for someone's attention—he could feel it in the pit of his stomach. He needed to get to Forestgrove—fast!

Aubrey walked up to the nearest receptionist and gently yanked the headset from her head. She paused in mid-sentence and issued a protesting, "Hey!"

"Listen," Aubrey overrode her complaint, "I need back up sent to Forestgrove Grocery ASAP, do you hear? This is an emergency—I may need an ambulance." He then grabbed a scratch piece of paper from the desk and scribbled down a few lines. "Here's the address."

"But all of our units—"

"I don't give two fucks where the units are. Get someone over to this address, pronto!" Aubrey barked, handed back the headset, and headed for the door at a trot.

Chapter 26

Alex was just starting to read the paper she had discovered to Aubrey when the phone had been knocked from her hand—perhaps that's too polite. In fact it had been *smashed* from her grasp by the impact of a ceramic catering tray, with such force that not only the phone was left broken once it hit the floor, but the tray shattered, sending fragments of ceramic to spew in all sorts of directions. It also broke Alex's hand and left it bleeding along the line of her knuckles.

Alex gave out a startled cry and moved backwards from the spray of shrapnel, cradling her hand protectively against her chest. With wide eyes she watched as Mr. Bartley stepped fully out of the shadows, and tossed the broken tray away. There was blood on the back of his hands as well and when he used one to toss back the loose strands of hair that had fallen into his face they left copper tints at the roots.

"Sorry, just had to stop that phone call." He smiled and cocked his head to one side, "I thought I told you to go home for the day." Nate took a step toward Alex, his smile wiped from his face so quickly she wasn't sure it had ever been there. She tried to back up as well, but found herself already against a wall of some kind.

"I'm sorry you had to be the one to find that note—I've been wondering where Sean put it—he had it just before I pushed him so hard he fell and broke his poor little cranium—HA! It must have fluttered the way papers do—like leaves on an autumn day, only the winds are never visible to the naked eye so we can't always predict which way they'll blow things." Nate shook his head and took another step forward. Alex tried looking around for an escape route or even a weapon of some kind to protect herself with. She needed to distract him—keep him talking until she could think of something.

"So you killed Sean because you were being fired? How is that fair?"

Obviously offended, Nate paused. Defensively he said, "It was Sean who informed the owners about my little gambling problem—and so what if I borrowed a few hundred bucks here and there to pay off my debts? I always paid them back! Not only that, but that little shit was going to be taking my place!"

"You were the one who stole that $500, weren't you?"

But Nate kept on talking like he hadn't even heard her, "Twenty years I've been running this God damn place. Twenty years dealing with those fucking rich cunts and their snooty husbands! And the Clivedales were going to let me go—just like that? I only had two more years until retirement! They promised to not press charges against me for the stealing—but they're keeping my pension as recompense—isn't that fucking fantastic?!"

Alex tried to make herself sound sympathetic as she tried to say, "Well, that is pretty harsh—" But Nate suddenly advanced upon her and placed both arms to either side of her shoulders, the palms turned into firsts as they ground themselves into the wall behind her. She noted how his breath smelt like whiskey and vaguely wondered if he hadn't been sneaking more than just cash.

"And then they send that young, condescending bastard to take my place? With his new ideas and his narrow focus of profit, Profit, PROFIT! That's all anyone ever fucking cares about these days! What happened to quality? To personal touches! To trusting, honest work! To letting a man retire and give up his throne gracefully, not yanking it out from under him!"

Suddenly Nate's voice grew quiet, and for once during his speech he looked at Alex as if realizing she was really there. The candor with which he spoke his next line raised the hair on Alex' flesh. "I really am sorry you found that letter. Now I'm going have to kill you too."

Alex tried to wave off the whole thing like it was no big deal with her uninjured hand, "No-nnnn-no you really don't have to! I won't tell anyone, I promise!"

"Promises aren't worth two shits nowadays." He grabbed her shoulders then and frowned, "I'll have to make it look like an accident though."

For a moment Nate was silent, but then the smile crept back onto his face like a snake that had just recently feasted and he said, "I know, how about I throw you into the box crusher?"

Alex felt herself turn cold as she had a mental picture of being crushed alongside Daily Bread and banana boxes, with bones broken out of the skin, blood everywhere. . . She then experienced a slight vertigo and probably would have slid to her knees if Nate hadn't been holding her up.

Her breathing and heart rate had accelerated, but she wasn't aware of her surroundings until Nate began to jerk her weight back toward the Receiving Area, to the box crusher, and to her certain death. Luckily for her, that's when the adrenaline kicked in.

She suddenly dropped to a dead weight, causing Nate to stumble forward and releasing one shoulder so he could catch himself from falling. With her good hand now free she dug into her apron pocket and pulled out the first thing her fingers grasped and stabbed him in the chest with it.

Nate cried out and cursed as he took a few steps backwards. She hadn't grabbed her car keys like she had wanted, but the paper mate pen had mostly the same effect. Luckily for her, Nate's shirt had been slightly ballooning as he had been bent over, so she was able to wedge her weapon into an open area where the two sides of a shirt meet, just above a button hole.

But her accomplishment was only a minor one. The fact that it had been a pen had been good because it had better reach, but her thrust had been weak and it wasn't enough to stop the man with the killer gleam in his eyes. He pulling the thing out and rushed back for round two; however, it had bought her enough time to get to her feet and make a run for it!

Nate's bustle was blocking her route to Receiving and the back door, but Forestgrove Grocery was a giant circle, and past the mop closet was the entrance to the produce cooler, which led to the produce packaging area, and to a second door which led onto the sales floor—this one being the closest to the front entrance!

Alex ran as fast as she could, losing her hat along the way and using her shoulders and hips to bang through the cooler doors as she once again cradled her broken hand against her chest. It was beating so fiercely with pain that it felt as if she had a second heartbeat and this one felt like it was about to have an attack.

She didn't look behind her as she bolted for the front doors, and her ears were overcrowded with her own laborious breathing so she couldn't hear any sounds of pursuit. Carelessly she knocked over an orange display—an intense tackle that would have made any Packer fan proud, but didn't take the time to consider the hilarity of the situation. Instead she hoisted herself up, her eyes breaking with tears at the raw pain in her hand, since she had used it to help cushion her fall, and continued on her way, grapevining through the orange minefield.

She hit her first brick wall as she reached the front doors, large nasty red letters spelling NO EXIT painted on them. She knew that these letters lied, that if you could wedge one hand between the two doors, pushing one with a shoulder, and pulling the other with both hands you could make enough space to squeeze a body through—but her broken hand was useless, and the blood that had started flowing again made the doors slippery. The red letters seemed to sneer at her efforts.

Crying in desperation, praying to all the gods she could think of for assistance, she pushed and clawed at the one way doors with so much concentration that she never saw or heard the wine bottle soaring through the air until it conked her skull. Then all she saw and felt was a warm blackness, slowly covering her like a fleece blanket in wintertime.

Chapter 27

Aubrey slipped as he raced down the sidewalk to employee parking, trying to put on his jacket and run at the same time, cursed that no one had put salt down, and hurried the rest of the way through the snow drifts where he knew his footing would be surer. He didn't even pause to take the time to zip up his jacket or to fiddle with gloves and hat but made a straight line for the Dodge.

"Hang on girl," he said under his breath as he started his engine, "I'm coming. Just hang on."

Pulling out of the lot, Aubrey was relieved to find the majority of the populace were off the streets. That way he could have the whole road to himself and be able to skid into the wrong lane when needed. He thought about turning on the dashboard cherry light, but figured that if he removed a hand from the wheel for too long he might end up crashing into a parked car or tree—in which case, he wouldn't be any help at all.

Even so, Aubrey's driving couldn't have been considered 'safe.' Hanks would have been disappointed; professional stunt drivers might have been proud though. He plowed through intersections, speeding up if they were green to his favor, slowing down only if there were headlights to be seen coming from the crossing streets. He had to screech to a halt at a four way stop that met near the off ramp of a highway as it was filled with the last trickle of people trying to flee the storm like cockroaches suddenly put under a bright light. As he slammed on the breaks he fish-tailed back and forth for ten yards before coming to a complete stop, the nose of his truck only a few inches into the intersection, but he had kept his vehicle from spinning—that was the important part. He also drove over two curbs while making turns, cut across one person's lawn to avoid being stuck behind two cars that had wiped out and were now blocking his path, and just when he thought that he might never get there—up ahead loomed the shopping complex that Forestgrove Grocery happened to be a part of.

At first he hadn't seen it because their normally comforting glow of lantern light was missing. Glancing around he noted that the street lights in this area were also out and it was then that he remembered what Alex had said—the power was out.

As he pulled up to the hulking black figure that the brightness building made, and stranded his truck at an odd angle rather than parking it, he thought anxiously, *I just hope I'm not too late.*

The wine bottle used to hit Alex over the head did not break. It was a special vintage from Tuscany, made back in the 1890's, and Nate would have been sad to see it go in such a way. As he dumped Alex's limp form into a shopping cart (which he had gotten from the other side of the doors Alex had failed to open earlier, and which he himself had opened with no more difficulty then one might open a can that has a pull-tab already attached to it), he gently placed the bottle in with her, promising to set it aside to drink later in private celebration of his accomplishments.

While the bottle's glass hadn't even cracked, surprisingly enough, Alex's head hadn't shattered either. At the last second he had felt himself hesitate like a sentimental old fool, but there's no room for sentiment with murder and he made a pact with himself to never hesitate again.

Luckily for Nate, no blood flecked the floor, only the oranges which he could take his time picking up later. No, her skull wasn't cracked, but there was a large lump already puffing up the skin—one that would later scream HEADACHE—NEED TYLONOL! Nate grinned to himself as he thought of the mercy he would be doing this young doe. After being crushed to death, she wouldn't be feeling a thing.

"I'll show them, those Clivedales," Nate uttered under his breath as he started to push the grocery cart toward the back of the store. "I'll show them all! No one can run this place better than I can!"

The box crusher was located in a normally loud room that housed the furnace and other electrical equipment that kept the store operational. Because of the blackout, only a small amount of noise was ensuing, coming from the backup generator which seemed to wheeze like an old man. Nate gingerly propped open the entrance to this room and wheeled the shopping cart inside. He first removed the wine and placed it just behind the door so that he wouldn't accidently kick it and began unlatching the heavy iron door of the box crusher. Once that was opened he turned back to the cart and smiling at the still inert figure, began humming the *Snow White* classic "Whistle While You Work" as he moved forward to begin this last ghastly task of the day.

~*~*~*~*~

Alex was having a wonderful dream. She was swimming in the ocean and all around her were happy parents with their kids, toddling in the sand; barkers selling ice cream; and the best part—she was swimming with dolphins! The only strange fact which made it clear that she was dreaming, was that all the parents, children, and dolphins were oranges. But that really didn't matter. It also didn't matter that the water wasn't blue—but a deep merlot red, and the sky was green like new grass. It was a nice dream, even if it was close to a scene out of *Alice in Wonderland*—if only Alex's darn cat wasn't trying to nudge her awake! She wanted to stay in the warm water with the orange people and the orange fish. They wanted her to stay too, but now the cat was pushing her out of bed and it was making her friends slowly fade away. . .

"Stop it, you dumb cat!" Alex mumbled, but her mouth was dry and her words came out in a garbled mush. The cat kept pushing her and eventually Alex opened her eyes. She waited for what she thought was dream fog to float away, but eventually realized that her eyes were open and that she was hanging over the edge of something, staring into the abyss of a black pit. And it wasn't her cat pushing her into this yawning maw either, but the impatient hands of her psychotic boss. He had heard her meaningless drawl, and assuming she was soon going to wake up, had hurried his attempts at pushing her body into the crusher.

It was harder than he imagined it to be. Not only had he had to lift her from the cart, but lift her body a foot higher than that just to get her into the mouth of the damn thing. That workout alone caused sweat to start dripping from his forehead and made his breathing thicken. He was in good shape for a burly old man, but he was still an old man. Christ, he was almost 64 years old! He figured he deserved some kind of medal for pulling off a stunt like this at his age!

After he had finally gotten her limp form onto the shelf of the crusher, a sort of foyer before the main pit of it, her body somehow turned and wedged itself so that he couldn't push her any farther. He had to hoist himself partially into the machine in order to get that all straightened out. Even unconscious it was like she was still fighting him, the bitch! And to make matters worse, now she was waking up.

Realizing her situation, Alex tried to turn her body around, to find a purchase of some sort that might postpone the fall that was about to happen, but there was nothing she could grab turned the way she was, and with a final, hard shove from behind, she fell down into the stomach of the monster. As soon as she was amongst the few broken down pieces of cardboard she stood back up, trying to climb her way out. Her broken hand was forgotten by this new threat. Reaching out she was able to grab a hold of something soft— Nate's thinning hair which had again fallen into his face as he tried to pull himself out of the machine—and pulled. Nate yelped in pain, but batted away her hand easily enough.

"Get ready to die!" He called out as he freed himself from the contraption completely.

Alex instantly began to scream then, her panic so real she could hold it in her hands if they weren't shaking so much. Things like "No, please!" "I promise I won't tell!" "Help me, someone!" escaped her lips in pitiful cries like newborn pups looking for their mother.

But Nate's ears were deaf to her pleas of course, and to demonstrate this fact further he slammed the iron door and then pressed the green FORWARD button on the sooty console attached to the wall. Instantly it roared to life because it wasn't connected to the store's power grid, but to its own little generator that the box company had installed to go along with its horrid machine. They had warned him that it was dangerous—some kid had once crawled into an active one and he had been lucky enough to come out with just a few broken bones because of his small stature. But an adult? What could it do to an adult? Nate was entranced to see how his little experiment would go. If nothing else she would surely bleed to death—But wait, what was that?

Nate reluctantly turned his attention from the drama at hand and was annoyed as he recognized someone's voice shouting in the distance—and not a far distance either. Who could it belong to, this voice? All of the others had gone. He had made sure of that before he had gone to find that little cunt who was so casually reading his pink slip like one reads an ad in the paper. The detective, then? Could he have become alarmed and then come calling out of worry?

Like a spider, Nate picked up the wine bottle and crawled into the shadows behind the propped-open door to await his next victim.

Chapter 28

Aubrey had to forcefully push open the doors to enter the building. He paused at the second set of doors. There was some sort of emergency lighting on, causing anything it touched to be diluted in a copper-like glow. It may have distorted the colors on whatever it caressed, but it also made the dark streaks on the windows of the doors clearly visible. "Those look like bloody finger prints. Shit!"

Without waiting, thinking he might already be too late, he forced open the second set of doors and was perplexed to find a bunch of oranges all over the floor. *Some sort of struggle,* he observed. Stepping around them he unholstered his gun, but kept it aimed at the floor. He didn't want to have to use it if he didn't have to. *That would be another set of papers I'd have to fill out.*

To hell with the papers! Shut up and focus!

Right, sorry.

"Hello? Anyone here? Alex? This is Detective Aubrey Steiner of the Sheboygan Police Department. Is anyone here?"

But no one answered—at least no one human. As soon as the call left his mouth, a machine's gears somewhere at the back of the store started moving, causing a deafening sound in the otherwise, almost silent place. The sound sent a chill up his spine, but he pushed away his instincts of flight and pushed onward, calling out as he went, "Hello? Police officer—is anyone here? Alex, where are you?"

~*~*~*~*~

After Nate had slammed the door in her face, Alex stumbled and landed hard on her left side, down into the depths of the box crusher once again. The edge of a box sliced her inner arm, like a thicker version of a nasty paper cut, but otherwise the cardboard acted as a sort of cushioning—at least she hadn't landed on the hard metal itself. There was a seam leading to the outside world that provided some sort of luminosity as well as bringing in the chill and some stray flakes of snow. She was able to see the opening that she was pushed through only three feet above her—probably no more difficult to climb into than mounting a horse on a merry-go-round.

Her original plan was to plead with Nate to stop, that she wouldn't tell his secret—not necessarily to try and divert him back to sanity—he was way past that point now, but to try and give her some more time to gather herself together and find a way to escape. But then Nate had pushed the FORWARD button and Alex's surroundings began to vibrate. The wall closest to her head started to slowly move toward her. That's when her first true screams began.

The wall was moving toward her too quickly to try and climb out. Crying, she crawled as far away from the oncoming threat as she could until she felt the condensed cardboard stacked behind her. She tried to claw a hole into them, not feeling the thin slices the cardboard corners left along her arms, but the stack was as solid as a brick wall. There was nowhere else to go. The seam to the outside was too narrow for anything more than a hand to fit through, which she did in the final weak attempt at gaining someone's attention. But deep down she knew no one was out there. There wouldn't be any passerbys to hail, no witness to her murder, or "accident." She would die being turned into a cube and all because some lunatic wasn't ready to retire.

When Aubrey pushed through the Receiving Area

doors he used too much force and they banged against their door stops, but still he kept going, this time his call kept silent and with his gun raised. The grinding noise was coming from an open doorway, slightly blocked by a shopping cart. He thought he could also hear something else amongst the groaning noise but couldn't place it. Once he recognized it for what it was—the screams of a desperate woman—he ran forward, no longer being cautious, pulled the cart out of the way (it zoomed backwards and ran into something with a loud crash) and entered the electrical room. He passed his gun to his left hand and with his right opened the door to the box crusher. The screams became un-muffled and battered his ear drums like nails being drawn against a blackboard.

Aubrey turned toward the console on the wall and pressed the big red button, not even seeing that it read TO HALT A CYCLE, but relying on the instinct that green means go and red means stop, learned back in kindergarten. The machine stopped instantly and was silent; so did the screams dwindle down to a hyperventilating whimper.

It was then that Aubrey decided to allow himself a sighing breath, and it was also then that Nate rushed him from the shadows with the wine bottle raised above his head. This time Nate didn't hesitate, and not only did the bottle hit flesh (Aubrey's hand which dropped the gun, making it go off—the stray round embedding itself into the backup generator which began to have a seizure of blue electrical light) and draw blood, but it slammed into the wall beyond, this time shattering into jagged edges. Wine spewed and took solace in anything it could easily soak into. Nate still held the nose of the broken bottle, now brandishing it like a knife, and came dancing at Aubrey, this time for the kill.

Aubrey did his best to dodge the swings, all the while waiting for an opening. He felt a sharp pain as the bottle sliced him across his chest, hard enough to rip his shirt and start a thin trickle of blood to start oozing down his front. He veered sharply from another thrust and came away unscathed, but he had underestimated the old man's speed and wasn't able to side step the swipe to his right calf which was a direct hit, instantly making him fall to his knees. The only good thing about the attack was that it was low and caused Nate to become unbalanced. Aubrey was able to tip the scales by tackling his legs and lunging on top of him. Protecting his face, Aubrey finally managed to get the broken bottle away from Nate, but then Nate bit the fleshy part of Aubrey's hand, stealing the weapon back.

They broke away for a minute, both panting and watching each other—waiting to see who would make the next move. Aubrey, closest to the exit but not planning on running away or letting his man escape, moved into a crouch, leaning his weight on his good leg. Nate had a massive nose bleed and used a shirt sleeve to wipe the worst of it away. He stood up, a sick grin on his face. He was about to say something canny, but there was a thud and both turned in time to see a startling sight:

Alex, bruised, battered, and bleeding had hoisted herself out of the box crusher and dropped to the floor. She picked up the forgotten gun and aimed it at Nate. Her hand was shaking and she used her damaged one to help steady it.

Aubrey smiled, grateful that she wasn't dead. In his cop voice he said, "Drop the bottle, Nate. It's over."

Nate ignored Aubrey all together and charged Alex. There were no clear thoughts running through his head anymore, just the emotions of rage and jealousy for everything out of which he was ever cheated.

Alex fired the gun until all the rounds had been

expelled. The first two were total misses which ricocheted in different directions and embedded themselves into the first soft thing they encountered. One hit Aubrey in his already injured leg. He let out a fresh cry of pain and crashed to the floor. But the last three in the chamber made their mark—Nate's chest. He jerked with each shot, blinked in confusion, and slowly sank to the ground.

But even after Nate was no longer a threat Alex continued to pull the trigger, aiming the gun at his now inert form; gentle clicks sounding with each tug of her finger.

Aubrey ignored the raw fire tearing up his leg and crawled over to her. At his approach she jerked the gun in his direction, but stopped making it fire. "It's alright, Alex. It's over now. Give me the gun, please."

Alex's eyes were wide, broken open by tears. She suddenly felt tired and found she couldn't stop shivering. She let Aubrey take the gun away and watched as he jammed it into the back of his waistline, then quickly caught her as she nearly collapsed from adrenaline overdose. They sat that way for a while on the cement floor, Alex sobbing into Aubrey's wine and blood stained clothes while Aubrey stroked her hair. They were completely oblivious to the fact that the lights had come back on.

Alex uttered something and Aubrey pulled slightly away to hear what it was.

"I can't work here anymore. I quit!" She declared, sounding so much like a four-year-old that Aubrey had to bite his tongue to keep from laughing. But she could feel his whole body shaking with amusement and after awhile she joined in and they both laughed and cried in each others arms until the first backup unit found them that way with Nate's corpse just a few yards away—a perplexed expression still stamped on his face.

Chapter 29

Alex's hospital room was comfortable enough, but after three days of being bedridden she was getting restless. Thanks to her horror of a Valentine's Day, she had come away with a hand broken in three places, a concussion, a sprained ankle, two broken ribs, and multiple small cuts and bruises. She was also more tired trying to recuperate here than she felt she would be if they would just let her go home—what with all of the friends, family, doctors, nurses, policemen, and media trying to sneak in—but the doctors had been persistent. The morning nurse had hinted that today might be the day of her liberation, but that had been four hours ago and Alex was becoming pessimistic.

At least the hospital stay was a free ride thanks to the Clivedales who insisted upon paying all of her hospital bills. It was a great relief that they had taken full responsibility for their ex-manager gone insane instead of Alex having to call up a lawyer and go about it all in an expensive, legal way. They had also settled upon a separate settlement which Alex was sure she couldn't have obtained even if they had gone to court. The only thing she did not take from the Clivedales' offer was a manager position at their future restaurant venue which would eventually take the place of Forestgrove Grocery.

That's right—the grocery store was to be no more. Freddy the Ferret was to be put to sleep, the whole place gutted and refurbished into a fancy Italian style restaurant. With all of the death and villainy out in the open, the Clivedales thought it best to start afresh—besides, everyone likes a good lasagna, right?

A few of Alex's co-workers came to visit her in the

hospital the day before and had brought along this surprising news. What was more surprising was that most of them were going to stay. The Clivedales owned more than one business in the area and, while the grocery store was being renovated, the employees who wished to stay with the company were given raises and sent to help out at the other establishments until the new restaurant's grand opening. Even with a total face lift, Alex wasn't sure if she could enter that building ever again. So far she couldn't even sleep with the lights off.

Alex would have to find some sort of job soon, but for now she was happy to be unemployed and with enough money in the bank to supply her needs for a while. . . unless she used it to—

There was a soft knock on the door frame and Alex was snapped out of her reverie to find a stunning, but shy Bobby filling the doorway. Instantly Alex perked up, a smile set pleasantly on her face.

"Hey, Alex. How are you feeling?" he asked, coming further into the room. There was a vase of tiger lilies in one hand, and a gift shop bear with the words "Get Well Soon" stitched upon its stomach in the other. He set the flowers on a night stand and handed her the bear. "I'm sorry I didn't visit you earlier, but I didn't know it was *you* who was in the grocery store skirmish until I met up with Tim and some others. I came as soon as I heard!"

Alex laughed, "Yeah, unfortunately that was me. I'm doing a lot better. I'm supposed to be going home today, so it's good you came when you did."

There was the sound of someone clearing their throat coming from the doorway. Alex looked over, but didn't recognize the person standing there. Bobby quickly waved the guy in and explained, "Hal, this is Alex, the girl I was telling you about who makes the best burgers in the world!"

"I don't know about that. The whole world?" Alex asked playfully.

The guy named Hal came in and slipped an arm around Bobby's waist and said, "Nice to meet you. Hope you're doing better."

"Alex, this is my boyfriend, Hal. I've wanted you to meet him for awhile."

The sparkle in Alex's eyes died right then and there, but she managed to keep a smile to her lips, "Nice to meet you too. And, um, thanks for the flowers and the bear. It's really cute."

There would have been a very uncomfortable moment if Alex hadn't pretended to stifle a yawn and say with a sleepy voice, "Oh, I'm sorry. I guess I'm still pretty exhausted from everything. It's been a very long week."

Bobby took the hint, "Alright, well, I really am glad you're okay. And it's a pleasure to know that one of my friends is an A class hero. See you around?"

"Of course," Alex said. They exchanged goodbyes and the two boys left. End of visit.

Most of her visits had been similarly short. Unless of course they were with close friends like Jacquelyn or Sue, but once they entered Alex's room and saw the bandages and bruises, people became shy pretty fast.

Alex had been sad to learn from Sue that Evan had indeed been arrested for theft. His first court session was sometime next week. And that Cyndi was basically heartbroken and had become a recluse. From Jacquelyn she had heard more jovial tales about how Parker was going to be in charge of wait staff for the new restaurant, Larry Duke was already planning a suitable menu, Julie had decided she would enjoy playing hostess, and poor emo-kid Spencer had been deemed head dishwasher. Alex wondered if he would ever get out of that rut.

Jackie, the florist, declined the Clivedale's offer and transferred to a Piggly Wiggly where her creative displays were greatly welcomed. Claire decided to become a stay at home mom and had left the retail world completely, and as for Jacquelyn, she found a job as a full time receptionist for a local insurance company. Timothy was doing a job search of his own by looking at possible prospects back in Chicago, the wedding jitters becoming a reality as the date drew nearer (Alex still had no idea what to get them for a wedding present). Meanwhile, Daniel decided to take a break from working life before going off and fulfilling his dream of becoming a pastor (or whatever they call it).

As Jacquelyn continued on about who was going off to do what, Alex's heart had felt heavy. The world she had known, the family she had been apart of was slowly eroding away and there was nothing she could do to keep them glued together. Maybe if she hadn't stumbled upon that stupid pink slip, then none of this would have happened.

But if she hadn't stumbled upon the missing piece of the puzzle, then what would have happened? Nate would have blown up eventually, maybe even killed someone else, and perhaps no one would have noticed . . . at least that's what the residential shrink said.

Alex closed her eyes, trying to keep tears from rising to the surface. Her world had been slowly falling apart ever since Sean's death, only she hadn't been prepared for such a sudden and intense change. And her crush, Bobby, was gay. There was nothing she could do about that either.

Suddenly another knock sounded at the door, this time more confident and playful. Alex opened her eyes to a smiling face that she was beginning to love to see.

"Afternoon, beautiful," Aubrey said as he walked further into the room—or rather, he limped. The bullet that had entered his leg as well as the gash suffered by the broken bottle had weakened him enough that he needed a cane to help support himself, but at least nothing life-threatening had resulted from the scuffle with Mr. Bartley.

"Are you supposed to be up and walking around so much?" Alex asked. Aubrey had been issued a room a few doors down, and even with his injuries he had managed to be Alex's most frequent visitor.

"I get stir-crazy if I sit too long. Besides, I come from a 'rub dirt in it' kind of family, and the best way to treat a wound such as this is to walk it off."

Alex rolled her eyes, "Sure it is."

With a slight look of agony, Aubrey pulled a chair closer to the bed and took a seat. "I just heard they're going to release you today. The nurses are gathering the outpatient paperwork as we speak."

Alex let out a sigh of relief, "Thank, God. I'm beginning to go crazy in here myself. The heart monitor thing is driving me nuts and there's nothing good on TV."

"And I'm sure you're looking forward to a real meal, huh?" Aubrey grinned.

Alex laughed, "Actually, hospital food isn't that bad. Their meatloaf is wonderful."

"Hmm, I took the chicken option that day, and believe me, it was nothing to squawk about."

They were silent a moment before Alex inquired, "Hey, I forgot to ask earlier, but did your supervisor ever apologize for closing your case prematurely? When they were trying to take my statement my second dose of morphine was over due and I was kind of bitchy—but I put in lots of quips about what a good job you did, and that if it hadn't been for you I'd probably be dead right now, stuff like that."

Aubrey chuckled, "Yeah, Helmer mentioned what a spit-fire you were, but I didn't exactly get an apology—big men don't ever really give those. I did get a pat on the shoulder, a 'good job, son,' and a hint at a promotion of some sort."

"That's it!? He should be groveling at your feet for what you did!"

"Yeah, well, it won't matter much in the long run. Honestly, I'm just happy you're safe. Which reminds me, not tomorrow, but in a week or two, when it's convenient, would you mind going with me somewhere?"

Alex paused for a second before asking, "Going where? Like on a date?"

Aubrey waved his hands, "No, not a date exactly. I just want to do something for you, as a sort of thank you. And I don't want to tell you what it is because I want it to be a surprise. Otherwise you might cut out at the last second."

"Hmm, I don't know. This seems a bit sketchy," Alex mused.

Aubrey stood up slowly, "Going with a police officer is sketchy? Especially a top rate one like me?"

Alex laughed, "Fair enough. I'll give you a call once I

get settled. Will I need anything where we're going?"

Aubrey shrugged, "Just an ID." He started shuffling back toward the door. Halfway there he turned around again and added, "Oh, and you'll need to wear something fancy—a step or two above business casual."

"Yes Sir, Detective Steiner, Sir," Alex saluted.

Chapter 30

It was two weeks after the horrendous event at Forestgrove Grocery and although she still had nightmares about the box crusher and now had to cope with claustrophobia issues, Alex was feeling pretty good. Her left hand was in a cast, she had a yellow-green bruise that peeked just a little bit past her hairline, and the rest of her was a collection of minor healing cuts and bruises, but she felt these only made her look more fabulous in her blue cocktail dress with the black lace edging. She figured Aubrey would be impressed when he picked her up for their "date" any minute. At least he better be—that zipper was a pain in the ass to manage with only one hand and she didn't even want to think about how she was going to get the blasted thing off again later.

He arrived a few minutes after Alex had added a touch of makeup to her bruise, and WOW did he look good in his five-piece suit—even with the cane he was instructed to use while his leg finished healing. The jacket and pants were jet black, his vest a steely grey, his undershirt an off white, and his red tie had a diamond stick pin to pull it all together.

During their initial greetings, Alex's cat sauntered over to the doorway and took his place next to its master. His golden eyes seemed to give Aubrey the once over and the casual way he turned his head toward Alex suggested his approval.

Both Alex and Aubrey fought back smiles as they watched this display, but finally Aubrey said sheepishly, "Your cat seems nice, but I'm actually more of a dog person."

The cat lifted up its nose and walked away again, approval denied.

Getting back on track Aubrey exclaimed with a full smile on his lips, "You look amazing."

Alex stammered, "Thanks. You look pretty sharp yourself. Are you sure this isn't a date?"

Aubrey didn't answer, but instead took her by her good arm and directed her to his truck. After doing the gentlemanly thing of opening and closing her door, Aubrey got in from the driver's side and helped her with the seatbelt. "Are you curious about where I'm taking you?" It was his turn to be playful.

"I'm curious that you won't tell me even if I ask you."

They were both smiling as they pulled away from the curb and headed through the city streets. Alex looked out the window, watched as chunks of ice floated down the gutter rivers to their unknown sewer destinations.

"You would scarcely believe that just a little while ago this whole place was covered in ice and snow so thick that plows were getting stuck!"

Aubrey mused, "That's Wisconsin weather for you. A shit storm one day and weather in the high fifties the next. So did you find yourself another job yet?" Aubrey inquired.

Alex shrugged, "Actually for now I'm enjoying being unemployed. The Clivedales feel responsible for what happened, as they should be. They're insisting on paying my hospital bills which is nice. They also offered me a management position at one of their restaurants, but I declined. I have an idea of sorts forming of what I'm going to do with the settlement money I'll be getting, so we'll see what happens."

They were silent for a moment, but Alex added quickly, "Oh! I forgot to tell you that Bobby came to visit me on my last hospital day. You should have seen him! He didn't know it was me who was a part of that whole gun shooting thing and when he found out he bought me the largest bouquet of flowers and the cutest little bear."

"I told you he liked you. Did he ask you out? Better yet, did you ask him?"

Alex fiddled with her fingers a bit. Some of the feeling was returning to the tips of her broken hand, and little tendrils of pain shot up her arm. "He came in with his boyfriend attached basically at the hip. I told you that boy was gay."

Alex smiled as Aubrey said with a chuckle, "Not going to lie, but I'm glad to hear it." He took one hand off the steering wheel so he could squeeze Alex's right hand. "Although it makes me worry all the more that once I leave for California, there won't be anyone to keep you out of trouble."

"California?"

Aubrey replaced his hand on the wheel to make a turn and nodded, "That's one of the reasons I wanted to take you out somewhere. I wanted to tell you that I'm leaving the area. I put in my transfer request and I just found out yesterday that I'll be heading to California to start my career with the undercover narcotics squad in LA in just a few weeks."

"But why—"

"Because of you," he paused to look at her face.

Returning his gaze to the road he said, "It's sort of a long story. See, my father always wanted me and my brothers to become cops—but me especially because I was the oldest son. And because I have what he calls 'The Steiner Sonar' which is like these weird gut feelings that supposedly all Steiner men get. Personally I think its just gas most of the time, but with your case and—and with the one I was a part of last fall, I know that at least half of what of my old man was saying is true."

"What happened last fall?"

"I'm getting there. But first, when you met me you called me an alcoholic. And at first I thought you were full of shit, but the more I thought about it, the more I knew you were right. And at that point I hated the job, I hated the fact that I had failed my family, and I felt like the only way to be a cop is to be the bad guy. I had lost sight of what matters most about being a policeman—not the paperwork, or putting away the bad guys (not that those aren't important too), but listening to your gut and to the details of what's going on around you. To help the lives or even just one life of an individual who needs you—that's what it means to be a cop. To help the people who can't help themselves."

Aubrey paused and Alex noticed that they had left the city limits and were now traveling on rural roads. After a deep sigh he continued, this time more somberly, "You helped me realize that I was in a rut and that I needed to do something to get out of it. So for that, I thank you. The rut itself formed because of what happened last fall, and not too many people know my side of the tale other than what I put down in my official statement.

'So last fall I was working with the narcotics unit down in Milwaukee. This whole part of the state is a druggy's paradise. If we take out one drug lord, by the next month two more are at work, sharing the old one's territory. Well, I was a part of an undercover ring, and I got in pretty deep, pretty fast. Once my position was secure, my job was to monitor the movements of the gang leaders and find an opportune time when my boys could storm in and take them out.

'We got the date set, and I was ready to give my guys on stakeout the signal to move in once the big boss showed up to this crack party, but all day I had this funny feeling in my gut that something was going to go bad; that I should just walk away from this one.

'It was getting late and the head honcho still hadn't arrived. Then, about 1 a.m. he finally showed up, but he wasn't alone. He had my baby cousin under his arm. When they arrived, she was so drugged up she didn't even recognize me—and all of us kids were thick as thieves all the way through middle school! That was the first time in my career where I froze. I didn't know what to do, I mean, she was kin and I had no idea she was doing that kind of stuff! Christ, she was just a sophomore in college that year at UWM!"

Aubrey's voice had become ragged and he paused to compose himself. Meanwhile the truck turned onto a gravel road which advertised to be some sort of campsite, but Alex didn't catch the name in time. All she saw was a sign made up of a silhouette of a bear, possibly with an arrow sticking out of its back. There was a dense crop of trees on both sides for some time. Then the trees broke away to reveal three buildings; two made to look like log cabins, and the third was made of concrete. Aubrey parked close to the cement building but kept the engine running to keep the cold at bay. The snow might be melting, but it was still chilly outside.

Once parked, he turned to Alex and finished his story,

"So right before I could decide between family or career, she recognized me. At first she was all over me, hugging and kissing like she hadn't seen me in years even though we saw each other in July. Then she stops very suddenly and pulls away from me like I've bit her because she realizes that I'm a cop. . . dressed in plain clothes. . . at a crack party. We stared at each other for maybe two seconds before she screams "COP!" at the top of her lungs. Next thing I know guns are being pulled out of all sorts of places and people start swearing and yelling and shooting. My guys on standby pick up on the crazy shit that's going on inside that house and storm the place. We ended up arresting the big boss and his right hand man. There were some others there wanted for minor felonies and some with unregistered guns. Overall it was a good haul, a job well done."

"And your cousin?" Alex pressed gently.

"She was one of the first ones shot in the chaos."

It was Alex's turn to put a comforting hand on his arm, "I'm sorry, Aubrey."

But Aubrey just shook his head, trying to clear away the visions that had resurfaced with his story. "Now you know why I started drinking—to keep the ghosts at bay. See, my family didn't just see a cop doing their job—except maybe my father—especially my aunt and uncle, they just saw someone who betrayed their family and have been shunning me ever since. After the incident I transferred away from the narcotics unit. I figured that if I had to be a part of death like that I should just be a homicide detective, that way it would all be up front and I wouldn't have to pretend to be someone else. But that didn't work either. Being around home just stirred the pot for my family even more, and working with my dad's old buddies made me feel like a school kid all over again. They wouldn't let me off the leash until I got a hold of the Ritter case and by then I had basically stopped caring."

"So you think moving to California will make a difference?"

"I think it's a start yes. I need to break away from my father's influences. Even though he's been gone from the precinct for almost five years, his name gets dropped in my ear almost twice a day! It's hard living in that man's shadow. I need to know if I have what it takes to stay in police work using only my own two feet—and maybe a little 'Steiner Sonar.' "

Alex nodded, "I see your point. Promise you won't forget me though?"

Aubrey laughed, "Oh, I have no intention of doing that. In fact, now that I have your phone number I'm going to harass you to harass me to behave out there in Cali. I plan to be stone sober as long as I'm away and I'll need you to make sure I stay that way."

"I can do that," Alex promised, then laughed gaily as she pointed to the building they were park next to. "So, where are we?"

~*~*~*~*~

Alex's question was soon answered as they entered the building, signed in using Aubrey's membership, picked up some gear, and then were shown to their own private section of the shooting gallery.

"Today I'm going to teach you about gun safety."

Alex frowned, "Really? You do realize that my left hand is still in a cast."

Aubrey set the twin small handguns down on a table and began to dismantle the various parts in order to give a proper demonstration. "Rule number one: NEVER point the gun at another person if you don't know what you are doing. You might hurt someone innocent," He said in a mocking voice.

"Hey! I already apologized for accidently shooting you!"

"Yeah well, the bullet almost went up my ass, Hon. It's bad enough that I limp because of you. Can we start the lesson now, please?"

Alex glared at him, "You made me get all dressed up for this? I thought you were going to take me to a fancy dinner or—"

"Oh there's a reason you're dressed up and it's not just because I wanted to see you in a pretty dress. It is because," he picked up one of the unloaded guns, spun the barrel closed and made a striking pose, "It will be Bond, James Bond teaching the lesson this afternoon, and you my dear Miss Moneypenny, must know that a gun makes the finest sort of accessory if you'll let it."

Alex snorted through her fit of laughter, "Alright fine. You can be your James Bond and give me a lesson, but I don't want to be Moneypenny. I'd much rather get to stand up looking at the target and whispering my old favorite, *Go ahead punk, make my day!*"

Both were laughing so hard that the security guard in the room looked up from his paperback, only to lower it again with a wide smirk on his lips and a slight shake to his head which seemed to say, "Ah, young people. They're all crazy these days."

34104169R00109

Made in the USA
Middletown, DE
08 August 2016